THE INTIMATE MEMOIRS
OF AN EDWARDIAN DANDY

THE INTIMATE MEMOIRS
OF AN EDWARDIAN DANDY

Volume I

Anonymous

Carroll & Graf Publishers, Inc.
New York

First Carroll & Graf edition 1994

Carroll & Graf Publishers, Inc.
260 Fifth Avenue
New York, NY 10001

ISBN 0-7867-0107-2

Manufactured in the United States of America

THE INTIMATE MEMOIRS
OF AN EDWARDIAN DANDY

Introduction

RUPERT MOUNTJOY'S FASCINATING autobiography tells the story of a wealthy young Englishman whose adolescence and early adult life was spent first in the depths of the country and then among the cream of London Society around the turn of the century. It permits the present day reader to look backwards in time to when scions of the leisured aristocracy were able to devote their days and nights purely in pursuit of pleasure. Rupert Mountjoy sets down details of his own sybaritic life-style in frank, unexpurgated detail that gives weight to the arguments of those social historians who claim that a powerful current of sexuality surged beneath the repressed public morality paraded during these years.

Certainly we now know that it was members of the upper classes who ignored the almost hysterical thundering by the Church (then a more powerful social force than now) about the perils of sexual experience. From Rupert's diary (which would appear to have been kept as far as possible on a contemporary basis with the entries written down as soon as possible after the events described took place) we read, for example, of how the school chaplain Reverend Clarke railed against the harmless practice of masturbation. Interestingly enough, Rupert and his friends ignored these and other dire warnings about the Sins Of The Flesh and his memoir shows that a strict straight-laced public morality was challenged at both the top and bottom ends of the social scale.

Rupert describes his hedonistic life-style – enjoying huge luncheons after lazy mornings, followed by unhurried afternoons spent leafing through sporting magazines at the club, to be rounded off perhaps by a formal dinner party or by an evening at one of the popular West End theatres where outside, to complete matters, he and his cronies would visit one of the *maisons privées* to take their pick of the pretty girls available as bed-mates. This may well appeal to members of the vast majority of young men of Rupert's age living almost one hundred years later who have neither the time nor money to enjoy such a comfortable existence!

This is not the first publication of the Mountjoy adventures. Shortly before he was forced to decamp to the Australian outback by his irate father after a disastrous speculation involving the purchase of three racehorses in the late autumn of 1913, he wrote to his solicitors, the fashionable firm of Godfrey, Allan and Colin, instructing Sir David Godfrey 'to make the best financial use possible of my scribblings'. Sir David, himself known in London's clubland as a man of robust sexual proclivities, promptly sold Rupert's manuscript to the editor of an illicit magazine published by the notorious Cremornite fraternity for a sum that appeared to satisfy the most pressing of Rupert's creditors.

2

The Cremornites were a semi-secret band of rakes which included such well-known *roués* as the financier and friend of King Edward VII, Sir Ronnie Dunn; Max Dalmaine the writer and artist; Captain Alan Brooke of the Guards; and the suitably named Dr Jonathan Letchmore who appropriately enough makes a brief appearance in this narrative, which makes one wonder whether Ruper Mountjoy was not himself at least associated with the group in some way. Incidentally, this charmed clique took its name from the infamous old Chelsea park of Cremorne Gardens, which was closed down in the 1880s after many complaints about the rowdiness there that often ended with free fights spilling over into the Kings Road, after the bars closed. It was also one of the major venues for prostitutes to meet their clients, on a par with Leicester Square and Piccadilly Circus. Ostensibly, the Cremornites simply ran a dining society, but in fact their Mayfair headquarters was a known haunt for upper class men-about-town where discreet privacy was offered to participants in several recorded orgies that took place there in the presence of some of the highest personages in the country.

Rupert's personal confessions were serialised in the quarterly Cremornite journal through till 1917. Copies that were smuggled out to the trenches must have brought back wistful memories of happier days to the officers and men who faced the terrible slaughter of the Great War.

Luckily for Rupert, he was many thousands of miles away from the terrible conflict which was to spell the end of the kind of sybaritic luxury that we associate with the Edwardian era. From his letters to friends and family, it appeared that our author was in fact keen to enlist but was wisely prevailed upon to stay at home. He was influenced, one might surmise, by his fiancée, Nancy du Boute, to whom he was introduced shortly after his arrival in Australia. Also, the wheel of fortune turned in his favour in Sydney, even though his father, Colonel Mountjoy, had cut him off with only a second class one-way ticket to the New World and a cheque for £2,000. Rupert promptly invested this money in the establishment of a gentleman's club, the Odd-bods, in an elegant mansion just off Pitt Street, in the heart of Sydney. From all accounts it was based on very similar lines to the Cremornites' gatherings and, within a few years, Rupert was able to charge a hundred guineas a year as a membership fee. Nevertheless, the Club had a long waiting list of would-be members.

A few months after the Armistice in November 1918, a second unauthorised publication of Rupert's early diaries was printed in Manchester by the Society of Venus and Priapus, a circle about which little is known. In fact, scholars now speculate that the Society may never have actually existed but that it was simply a front for the spectacularly rude booklets printed under its name, probably by Oswald Knuckleberry of Didsbury, a great-nephew of Ivor Lazenby, the Victorian writer and publisher of such underground erotic classics as *The Pearl* and *The Oyster*.

In 1921 Rupert and his family (he married Nancy in 1915 and they produced three children, twin boys and a girl, within five years) emigrated once more to a new home, this time to a palatial ranch house in southern California. In a letter to his old friend, Sir David Godfrey, Rupert complains bitterly about the officers of the Sydney police force who he said were becoming too rapacious for the turning of a blind eye to the raunchy happenings at the Oddbods Club. And the Mountjoy family lived quietly in the sunny climes of California, with both Rupert and Nancy living to a ripe old age not far from the ultra-fashionable area of Beverly Hills.

There may be some who find Rupert Mountjoy's uninhibited writing somewhat shocking even today. But as Webster Newington, one of our foremost authorities on turn-of-the-century British erotica, has stressed, 'It must be noted that the underground publications of this time show that there existed a persistent questioning of the taboos which then existed and this sceptical attitude helped lead to the more relaxed self-understanding and enlightenment concommitant with the multiplicity of views on sexual relations which exist in the 1990s.'

Authors such as Rupert Mountjoy set themselves firmly against the authoritarian notion that mainstream sexuality was an area which had to be stringently controlled by the ruling Establishment, and it is timely that his writing has survived the years to be republished almost one hundred years later to provide an unconventional, irreverent insight into the manners and mores of a long-vanished world.

WARWICK JACKSON
Birmingham
February, 1992

I am fully aware that my youth has been spent,
That my get-up-and-go has got up and went.
But I really don't mind when I think with a grin,
Of all the grand places my get-up has been!

RUPERT MOUNTJOY
London
September, 1913

CHAPTER ONE

First Stirrings

LITTLE APOLOGY IS NEEDED – OR WILL BE made – for putting into print my frank, uncensored memoirs. For why should I not publish my diary? It may be of interest to both present and future generations of readers for many famous people are named in its pages. Here at the very start, however, I will freely admit to the alteration of certain names and places and the omission of a number of events, for nothing could induce me to embarrass or offend the sensibilities of any lady, from the parlourmaid positioned in the lower classes to the high and mighty London hostess who claims pride of place at the very apex of Society.

I trust you will appreciate my concern, dear reader, though let me hasten to assure you that the above *caveat* notwithstanding, I also confirm in clear type a matter of importance which I have stated verbally on numerous occasions to my close friends, whilst placing in order the many and tidying recollections from the disordered files of memory. I refer, of course, to the fact that every gentleman whose name appears in my memoir has happily granted permission for his nomenclature to be revealed. Several letters have reached me from old acquaintances of both sexes who, despite having been warned of my intention to write a candid and undisguised account of my recent past, have expressed their pleasure to hear of the project. Indeed, they have urged me not to leave out their names in my manuscript, whilst not hesitating to remind me of jolly times enjoyed together at St Lionel's or sampling the varied and often exotic delights afforded to gentlemen of means domiciled in the heart of Belgravia and Mayfair, surely the most propitious areas in London for those like myself whose chief interest lies in *l'art de faire l'amour*.

To complete these introductory words, may I cordially thank all who have assisted me in the compilation of what has turned out to be, according to my dearest chum Harry Price-Bailey: 'the horniest book of licking and lapping, sucking and fucking I have ever had the pleasure to read'.

So without ado, let us turn back the years to the summer of 1898 when I was a lad of just fifteen years of age, living with my parents at the family seat of Albion Towers, which lies near the sleepy little village of Wharton on the edges of the Forest of Knaresborough in Yorkshire. Few areas of Britain are so rich in beauty and interest as this part of the country. There are moors to hike across, several wooded valleys through which flow lovely streams with glittering falls, grand ruins of castles, abbeys and historic houses and many fine buildings which show few signs of the passage of time – all these and many other features of appeal are to be found on every hand.

This is why my father, Colonel Harold Elton Fortescue Mountjoy, late of the Indian Army, so enjoyed coming back to the home country after long service on the North West Frontier, for Yorkshire has an insistent appeal to all who delight in open-air pursuits, while the bracing air is unrivalled in England. Whilst the Pater busied himself with looking after our estate and taking every opportunity to go hunting, shooting and fishing, my Mama occupied herself with other ladies from the best families in the county. As surprisingly few houses were yet connected by telephone (I should add that we were an exception to this rule for though Father could be a bit of a crusty old buffer now and then, he was extremely interested in scientific progress and was the proud owner of one of Monsieur Lumière's cameras that could take moving pictures, but more of this anon) Mama spent much of her time writing letters regarding social events in our neighbourhood, from dinner parties for the gentry to trips to Harrogate with Lady Scaggers, The Hon Mrs Boote and other close friends.

We returned from India four years ago, leaving my elder sister Barbara in New Delhi where she lives with her husband, Lord Lisneigh, Deputy Governor of the North East Territories. However, though to all intents and purposes I was an only child, I rarely suffered from the pangs of loneliness. Although I had no companions of my age locally, I was at home only during school holidays for my education was conducted at the grand old school of St Lionel's College for the Sons of Gentlefolk far down south in the beautiful county of Sussex. There I made many pals

11

including some like Harry Price-Bailey, Terence Blacker, Clive Allingham and Frank Folkestone who have remained firm friends throughout the passing years. During our vacations we frequently visited each other's homes, and as Mama was always more than pleased to extend hospitality to my school-fellows, I spent few days without someone to pass the time with.

Nevertheless, I begin this excursion down the lane of recollection on one of these rare days. It was a glorious morning in early July 1898 and I looked forward to welcoming Frank Folkestone, the captain of the Upper Fourth at St Lionel's, to Albion Towers. Frank was spending the first week of the summer vacation with his parents at their home in St John's Wood before taking the train up to Harrogate where Papa and I would meet him. But what I hoped would turn out to be a highly satisfactory day opened on a gloomy note with the arrival of a telegram from Lady Folkestone, stating that Frank was suffering from a heavy summer cold and so she was postponing his trip up to us for twenty-four hours.

'It's only one day, Rupert,' said my Mama, trying to lift my spirits, 'and the weather looks so fine, why don't you spend the day out of doors? Perhaps you would like to join your father and Reverend Hutchinson who are fishing at the river on Mr Clee's land? I'll ask Mrs Randall to make you up a packed luncheon and I'm sure it will be in order for you to borrow one of your father's rods.'

But I declined the offer, for I have never possessed the patience to wait for a fish to take the bait at the end of the line. Still, the idea of spending the day out of doors appealed to me. An idea struck me – Mr Pilcher, the senior teacher of natural history at St Lionel's, had fired my class with the notion of starting a birds' eggs collection [*a practice now heavily discouraged – Editor*] and I thought that today would be as good as any to begin making up a set. I mentioned this to Mama who conveyed my request for roast beef sandwiches and a bottle of ginger ale to Mrs Randall in the kitchen whilst I went upstairs to change into an athletic vest and football shorts as the weather was uncommonly warm and I planned a three-mile hike to Knaresborough Woods.

So this is why, on that never-to-be-forgotten July morn, I went striding out of our front gates, my rucksack on my back filled with food for my *al fresco* luncheon and a woollen jersey to slip on in the unlikely event of a change in the weather. It was just after ten o'clock when I left home to walk through our grounds and as I walked briskly along, I had a vague sensation that someone was dogging my footsteps. Yet when I turned round to look behind me, which I did several times, the road was clear and I was apparently alone. I must be imagining it, I said to myself, yet there was no shaking off the feeling that someone was keeping pace for pace with me. The sensation of being followed is most disagreeable and I began to wonder whether some vagabond tinker was waiting to pounce upon me, though such crimes of petty robbery were so rare in the locality that any news of such a happening would warrant substantial coverage in the weekly *Harrogate Chronicle*.

Yet I could not rid myself of the notion that I could hear the patter of light footsteps that were not my own. But soon the path was clear of trees and though I was still a mite apprehensive, I was now also slightly ashamed of my first concerns. After all, the Queen's Highway was free to all and I was probably just being tracked for fun by a young son of one of the farmworkers whom my father employed to till our arable fields.

If anything, the sun now shone even more brightly. Soon after I crossed the meandering country lane that led to the Harrogate road I sat down to rest for a moment or two on a mossy bank. It stood on the verge of a meadow owned by our neighbour Doctor Charles Wigmore, whose sixteen-year-old daughter Diana was a girl whose beauty struck me tongue-tied and left me awkwardly attempting to remember my manners on the few occasions when we had found ourselves together in company. Momentarily a picture of the delightful Diana flashed across my mind as I allowed my rucksack to rest along the slope of the hillock and I stretched my arms and yawned, at peace with the world. I sat for a minute or two and then heaved myself up again – only to hear the quickening approach of another traveller behind me.

I turned to see that standing only some twenty yards away was none other than the lovely Diana Wigmore herself, also dressed for the heat of the summer in a white linen blouse and a similarly coloured dress which barely reached more than a couple of inches below the knees of her uncovered legs. She really looked the acme of feminine perfection, being a lovely rosy-cheeked girl with a gay twinkle in her bright blue eyes. She wore her tresses of light ash blonde hair gracefully pinned up around her graceful neck, and young and inexperienced though I was regarding the fair sex, her saucy little nose and pouting lips, together with the clearly visible heaving of her proud young breasts as she recovered from her sudden exertion, set my own heart pounding at a fair rate of knots.

'Good morning, Miss Wigmore,' I said shyly, congratulating myself on for the first time speaking to this gorgeous girl without stuttering or blushing furiously with nervousness. 'Have you been running to catch up with me? I thought there was someone on my trail but you kept yourself invisible every time I looked around to see who my mysterious follower could be.'

This time it was Diana whose face coloured up with genuine embarrassment. 'Oh Rupert, I do apologise – I know I should have called out to you at least a mile back. You looked deep in thought, and I thought it would be rude to disturb you.'

'I wasn't meditating about anything more important than how best to begin collecting birds' eggs for my collection. I haven't even started yet and I was only thinking as to whether I'd find anything in the nests at this time of the year.'

She smiled and a delicious dimple appeared on the side of her face. 'I don't know much about the habits of birds,' she said. 'Is your quest for schoolwork or simply for your own entertainment?'

'It's not very important at all – I just thought it a good excuse to get out of doors on such a fine day. I could have gone angling with my father

15

but, between ourselves, I find the sport boring though I know that many people derive much pleasure from the pursuit.'

Diana sighed and said: 'You are a lucky boy, Rupert. I have some holiday work which must be finished by the end of the vacation. As we are going on the Grand Tour next week [*a favourite summer trip by English families to Italy that usually encompassed Venice, Florence and Rome – Editor*] I must complete my portfolio to gain the certificate in art which I need to go on to further studies at college next term.'

'I didn't know you were an artist, Miss Wigmore.'

'Oh please call me Diana, Rupert. All my friends do – and you are my friend, aren't you?'

'I would love to be,' I said boldly, 'and I just wish there was something I could do to help you in your work. But I can hardly draw a straight line and I know very little about painting!'

'But there *is* something you can do, Rupert, though I hardly dare ask you,' she burst out.

'Well, if we are friends, you should be able to ask anything of me – all I can promise is to do my best to oblige. But if I cannot help I will just say so and nothing is lost.'

'You *are* a sweet boy. Very well then, I will take up your offer but promise me you won't be too shocked and that, whatever happens, you will keep this conversation secret,' she demanded.

'I give you my word,' I said, puzzled by the earnest look on her pretty face. 'This must be a matter of very great importance to you. So again, how may I be of assistance?'

Diana slowly expelled a deep breath. 'Rupert,

you might know that I attend Nottsgrove Academy, a progressive institution which believes in the equality of opportunity for women in both political and cultural matters. As far as art is concerned, Mrs Bickler, our art mistress, firmly believes that painters are often forced to suffer varying degrees of injustice from financial problems. This is due to a misunderstanding or dislike of their finest work by patrons or the ruling artistic establishment. For women, there has always been a further prejudice against which to battle which is why so few women have made any serious headway in this field.'

I listened patiently for even at this early age I had already realised the uselessness of interrupting when someone has climbed upon a hobbyhorse – and, anyhow, I enjoyed looking at this pretty girl who obviously cared passionately about her subject.

'There is still a bar against women at meeting places such as clubs or, heaven forbid, a genuine studio! Even at this early stage, I cannot find a subject for my figure studies.

'This is where I need your help, Rupert,' she added bluntly. 'I will not beat about the bush – I want you to pose for me whilst I make some charcoal sketches.'

'But that hardly seems an onerous task,' I declared, slightly puzzled by her words. 'Why, I'm truly flattered to be asked and I'd be delighted to help out. Look, I'm free this very minute if you would like to begin work straightaway.'

Her beautiful blue eyes sparkled. 'Oh Rupert, what a kind offer! Well, if you really mean it, just a half mile or so through that stile there is a

17

perfect place where I have set up my easel. On the ground lie my pencils and brushes. I've also brought along a small hamper, but Cook always packs too much and there'll be more than enough food for both of us.'

'It doesn't matter as I also have some sandwiches and a bottle of ginger pop in my rucksack.'

'Well, that would seem to settle it. You really mean it, Rupert? Shall we really start here and now?' she asked eagerly, seemingly surprised that I made so little of the matter.

'Why not?' I said gallantly and gestured for her to lead the way. As Diana had promised, we did not have far to walk before finding ourselves in one of the numerous interesting copses on her father's property through which ran several shady footpaths hidden from the view of any passer-by. Sure enough, she had set up her equipment on a blanket spread out on a level piece of ground where I dumped my rucksack.

'Here we are then,' she called out. 'It's such a pleasant day and the light is quite superb just now. Gosh, I can hardly wait to begin. Are you ready Rupert? Yes? Jolly good – we won't be disturbed in such a quiet spot. I suggest you get undressed over here and put your clothes on the blanket.'

I could not believe what I had heard and I looked at her in astonishment. 'What the deuce do you mean, Diana? Take off my clothes, did you say?'

She looked at me with a trace of impatience in her gaze. 'Yes, of course, my love, how else would I be able to sketch the male figure if not from an uncovered form?'

So this is why Diana was at first diffident about asking for my assistance! And why she was so happy to hear me consent to model for her without any fuss! I had assured her of my aid and it would be dishonourable and cowardly to break my word. I will readily admit that I could not bear to appear foolish in front of this gorgeous creature who, if I backed away from this challenge, would probably never deign to speak to me again! So I took a deep breath and said: '*All* my clothes, Diana?'

'Yes, dear,' she said steadily. 'Otherwise I would be unable to do either of us justice. So do be quick about it and then I'll show you just how I would like you to stand.'

I hesitated still. Sensing my modesty, she added encouragingly: 'Come on, Rupert, there's really nothing to it. Look, if it makes you feel any easier, I'll kick off my shoes and take· off this blouse and skirt. It's so hot that I'll feel far more comfortable just dressed in my chemise.'

I closed my eyes, for the dreadful thought flashed through my brain that if I even took the most fleeting of glances at the sight of Diana Wigmore clad solely in a chemise, it would be impossible to prevent my penis from instantly betraying my secret sensual desires. As it was, like all boys at this difficult age, I had little enough control over my prick which would swell up sometimes for no good reason and which demanded the attention of my closed fist at least three times a day. Still, I had no avenues of retreat, so I sat down on the stump of a nearby tree and removed my shoes and socks.

Then, drawing upon every ounce of valour in my body, I turned away and slipped down my shorts and drawers together and wriggling out of them, stood with my flapping white athletic vest covering just the upper part of my backside. I exhaled slowly before raising my arms and pulling off my remaining garment to stand totally naked in front of this amazing girl.

To her credit, Diana appeared to be unconcerned about her first sight of my bare body. 'Rupert, would you just lean back against that tree at a slight angle to the sun, but facing me full on. Good, that's absolutely how I want you. Lay your hands on your thighs and raise your head to the sky, no, not too much – there, that's right, can you hold that position? Are you comfortable? Now please keep as still as you can.'

I complied with her request and surprisingly soon the fact that I was standing in a state of complete nudity began to fade in importance. Diana chatted away as she worked, saying: 'Your body is well suited to a classical study, Rupert. You have the physique and more important, perhaps, the confident pose of a youth capable of surmounting all the obstacles which might occur in your life – not only through your undoubted physical strength but also by the sheer force of your personality. Now I have the talent, I want to capture that pensive look along with a clear-cut profile of your face with that proud look of determination stamped upon your brow.'

Her comments were perhaps slightly above my head but I felt flattered by all this attention and when, after half an hour or so, she suggested that we allowed ourselves a ten-minute break, I could hardly wait to pad over and see what she had committed on canvas. But before I could come round she placed her hand on my chest and said:

'Please, Rupert, wait till we have finished. You might not like what you see and whichever way you feel may adversely affect the way you pose for me afterwards. You don't mind, do you?'

'No, of course not,' I stammered, all too conscious again of my unclothed state and of the cool touch of her slender fingers upon my skin, especially when she let them trace a circular pattern around one of my nipples. 'You are so well proportioned for such a young lad. Why, you're almost as muscular as Roger, Lord Tagholm's son. My friends and I all much admired his manly torso when we saw him at the football club's gymnastic display last Easter.

'Naturally enough we never had a chance to see his powerful frame in such a glorious state of freedom, unburdened by superfluous vestments,' she murmured throatily, looking directly down at my perceptibly stiffening penis which was still dangling down but swelling inexorably, its ruby head already only semi-covered as I tried to prevent it jumping up to its full length. But despite all my efforts I felt my cock rise higher and higher, now fully uncapping the red-topped helmet as my shaft swelled up to its full eight and a half inches, standing smartly to attention against my belly.

My face turned bright crimson, for there was no way that Diana could have missed the swift rise of my tumescent tadger. Now a further shock awaited me, for I was certain that the lovely girl would toss her blonde tresses in disgust and at best walk silently away from me or, at worst, castigate me violently for being so rude.

I braced myself for the onslaught but to my

21

amazement, Diana moved her hand downwards to seize my shaft, and her long fingers, working as though they possessed a will of their own, started to frig my throbbing tool, rubbing it slowly, which made me almost swoon from the delicious sensations that coursed around my entire body.

Diana was delighted by my response and she said, really talking to herself: 'My goodness, what a splendidly proportioned penis for a mere lad. It looks so scrumptious that I would like to kiss it. But no, no, I must not let myself be so roused by this handsome boy and his immensely big prick. I really am very naughty to even touch it but I cannot help myself.

'Ah, how lewd,' she muttered as she drew back my foreskin, making my knob leap and bound in her hand. With her free hand, Diana unbuttoned her chemise and freed the uptilted, bouncy globes of her bosoms to my excited view. Now, I had peeped at French photographs of undraped females in the pages of *The Oyster* which Clee kept in his locker in our dormitory back at St Lionel's, but never before I had seen in the flesh the breasts of a pretty young woman. How tempted I was to touch those two proud beauties! And how well they were set off by the two cheekily pointed nipples, themselves each capped by the pink circles of the aureoles. The sweet girl groaned with unslaked passion as I plucked up enough nerve to move my hand up and gingerly tweak one of her engorged strawberry-like titties.

'Stop, Rupert, stop, you must be a good boy,' she murmured but I was in no mind to heed this plea and continued to feel her erect tittie with my fingers. 'No, I mean it, please stop that. I like it very much but we must get back to work. First, however, I'll finish you off which will give you some relief,' she gasped, gripping my twitching shaft even tighter.

Reluctantly I obeyed but she was as good as her word, as increasing the pace of her frigging, she rubbed my cock so sensuously that in a matter of moments the creamy froth shot out of my tool all over her fingers and splattered out over her chemise.

'Oh dear, I'd best take off this chemise and wash it in the stream. I'll have to do the same with my knickers, as they are already wet with my juices. If I don't, our laundrymaid is bound to gossip with the other servants about the state of Miss Diana's underclothes,' she said lightly. The thought of seeing this exquisite girl strip off her remaining garments set my truncheon standing up to attention again from its state of semi-erectness it had subsided into when Diana had finally relinquished her grip.

'Now, now, Rupert, behave yourself!' she grinned, ordering me back to my tree with an imperious wave of her arm. I sighed but trudged back obediently as Diana called out: 'I tell you what, my family only sent you a boring old book for your birthday last month. If you will try to stay as still as you can, in the same way as you managed before, I'll give you a very, very nice late birthday present before lunch which we'll both enjoy even more that we did just now.'

A late birthday present, I mused to myself as I leaned back into my old position – what the blazes could she mean by that? Genuinely, I had not the slightest idea and even the sight of her licking her upper lip with the tip of her tongue failed to provide the clue to unlock the puzzle for me. Meanwhile, I had to concentrate both mind and body on holding my pose for this sweet lass, *la bella donna della mia mente** for Diana was a truly industrious worker and she stuck to her task, looking up and pausing only occasionally to ponder now and then for artistic inspiration. The minutes ticked away but I stayed as still as could be. To pass the time I thought of all the fun Frank and I would have after he arrived to stay with us tomorrow. I could just see his face when I told him about this current adventure! Wouldn't he just be green with envy when I told him about how Diana had wanked my cock! No, that's an unworthy thought I decided as, feeling weary, I shifted my weight from one foot to the other. On the other hand, I could tell him all about it without mentioning her name and ever letting on even if she and Frank were to meet at some later date.

'Okay, it's time for lunch,' sang out Diana, breaking into my reverie. I stretched my arms out and walked across to her, my excited gait showing her that I was ready and waiting for this special treat she had previously mentioned. She gave me a dazzling smile as she put her hands on my shoulders and said: 'Would you like your birthday present now, Rupert, or would you like to wait until after we've eaten?'

'May I have it now, please?' I asked humbly and she nodded her head. 'Yes, you deserve a nice present as you've been a very good boy and not tried to make me go further than I wanted.' Again, I was at a loss to understand her words

* The beautiful girl of my memory.

24

though now, of course, I realise that what she meant to convey was that I took heed of her request to let go of her tittie when it became plain that she really meant what she said.

Diana took hold of my arms and put them round her back, at the same instant moving forward so that we were now sweetly crushed together. She lifted her arms up to cradle my neck and bring my face to hers and our mouths met to join together in what was the very first kiss of passion I had ever experienced. I was totally engulfed in a torrent of idyllic bliss that swept in waves over me. I heard nothing, saw nothing and felt nothing but the ravishing excitement of this first embrace. Far from discouraging my roving hands, she herself moved them to her breasts and as I caressed the firm, rounded globes, she slid the straps of her chemise off her shoulders and I thrilled to the touch of her naked nipples that rose up like hard little bullets to greet me. My prick had already stiffened up to stand powerfully upright, as hard as a rock, my knob already burst free from its covering as the luscious girl grabbed hold of my straining shaft.

We were swept off our feet by this fierce outpouring of frenetic energy and we sank to the ground, still joined by our mouths with my right hand cupped around the jutting orbs of her breasts and Diana's fingers gripping my prick, ardently rubbing my shaft and now tonguing my mouth so vehemently that I could feel the boiling juices already fermenting in my balls.

The prudent girl sensed that I was nearing a spend and she swiftly withdrew from my mouth and rolled me over onto my back. Then suddenly her tousled blonde tresses were between my legs and her lips were upon my cock as she kissed the unhooded helmet, lapping up the blob of liquid that had already formed there and licking my purple mushroomed crown with her pink little tongue. She opened her lips wide enough to encircle my knob and instinctively – for of course my young penis had never before been placed in such a sublime haven – I moved forward to push my excited tadger even further into her mouth. 'A–h–r–e, A–h–r–e, A–h–r–e!' I panted as her magic tongue travelled wetly all over my tool. I thought I might even pass out from the unbelievable pleasure that scorched every fibre when her teeth scraped the tender flesh of my knob as she drew me in again between those luscious lips, sucking my shaft slowly from top to base, with her every sweet suction transporting me to even higher peaks of Elysian delights.

I groaned as I felt my balls hardening for I only wanted to continue this marvellous game. Diana looked up at my contorted face as I tried desperately to hold back the flow of sperm. The understanding girl promptly solved my dilemma by immediately freeing my twitching tool from its heavenly prison and she also withdrew her hand from my throbbing shaft.

Then with a saucy glint in her eyes she said: 'Well, you've unwrapped your birthday present, so to speak – let's see if you are old enough to know how to play with it.' And without further ado she climbed on top of me with her knees on either side, pulling open her love-lips with her fingers and massaging her pussey back and forth across the tip of my cock. I bucked and heaved,

26

wanting above all to slide my rampant rod into her cunt. She teased me for a moment or two but then she lifted herself before crashing down on my pulsating pole, tightening the walls of her cunney as she held me in place, rocking backward and forward, slicking my shaft with her juices as she rocked with ecstasy. This was simply too much to bear and as I pushed upwards once more I felt the white frothy spunk burst out of my cock. Diana screamed with joy as she too climaxed as the hot creamy spunk flooded into her and she shuddered with glee as I pumped jets of jism into her flooded crack. She leaned forwards, my now shrivelling penis still snugly inside her slit, and kissed me on my mouth. 'Well done, Rupert! That was a really splendid fuck,' she whispered in my ear as we lay panting with exhaustion.

As we rested, bathed in the bright sunlight, now entwined in each other's arms, I proudly mulled over the fact that I had now crossed the Rubicon and hopefully there would be many more opportunities to make further journeys with Diana. Naturally, like all of my contemporaries in the Upper Fourth, I enjoyed a daily five-knuckle shuffle. But I could never have imagined that real fucking could be so exciting and wonderful; it had surpassed all my expectations. Here I was lying on Nature's bed of grass, having made passionate love to the beautiful naked girl now in my arms. Or to be more accurate, having just had her make love to me! The tenderness of this first engagement will never fade from my memory. As the poet says, *me tamen urit amor; quis enim adsit amori.**

* Love consumes me yet – for what bounds may be placed on love?

Once we had regained our senses, we ate our luncheon with gusto, for the worship of Venus and Priapus fuels the appetite better than any medicine. 'I suppose you want to continue your drawing.' I said with a sigh as I collected up the detritus of our picnic and placed it in my rucksack.

'No hurry, my dear,' twinkled Diana as she took hold of my prick as I passed by, stroking the limp shaft until I felt the first stirrings of an erection.

'I don't know whether I can do it again,' I confessed, though the way my prick was swelling under Diana's ministrations appeared to leave little doubt.

'Just lie back, Rupert, and leave the rest to me,' advised my love with a gay smile.

Slowly at first she gently stroked the sensitive underside of my still-stiffening penis, allowing her fingers to trace a path around and underneath my balls which instantly made me tingle all over with an electric gratification. After a while she closed her finger and thumb around the shaft, sliding them along its length as her head dived down and, like a magic serpent, her tongue slid around and around my stiffstander until it was as hard as a poker and fairly bursting for action.

'M'm, I think you are now more than ready for the fray,' she murmured huskily, disengaging her lips from my pulsating prick as she rolled over on her back and motioned me to scramble up in front of her. I was on my knees in a moment, my cock just inches away from the gaping lips of her cunney that thrust through the silky mass of her blonde bush. I brought my straining stiff to the

28

charge and to our joint squeals of delight, fairly ran it through into the sopping depths of her warm, willing cunt until my ballsack swished against Diana's bottom. We lay quite still for a few moments as Diana's pulsing pussey squeezed my cock so exquisitely that for the second time I almost swooned away from the sheer pleasure of it all. She then heaved up her *derrière* and I responded to this move with a mighty shove of my own and we commenced a most exciting fuck. My rock-hard staff fairly glistened with her love juices as it worked in and out of her sheath, whilst the lips of her cunney seemed to cling to it at each time of withdrawal as if afraid it would lose its delectable sugar stick.

Our movements now locked themselves into a furious rhythm. Diana was transformed into a wild animal, screeching uninhibitedly as she writhed uncontrollably under me with the force of an approaching orgasm. I fucked her at an even greater speed until, with a little wail, she slumped backwards, her thighs clenched around my waist as her body shook in a rapid drawn-out series of spasms. Her cunney squeezed my cock even tighter and the pressure led very soon to me shooting off a further libation of sticky white seed inside her saturated love channel that drained my prick of every last drop of its precious elixir …

I have heard it said so many times that one's introduction to the joys of love-making can often be a traumatic experience and certainly it is a stepping stone into adulthood that one rarely forgets. First love can be tremendous – or absolutely disastrous. This usually depends upon the circumstances, on the partner of one's choice and to a very great extent, upon ourselves. I was naive, slightly shy and, at first, frankly bewildered by my first voyage along the highway of love but I was fortunate enough to be accompanied by a sophisticated girl who took the trouble to care for and cater to my every need.

Indeed, my heart was bursting with gratitude to Diana for her kindness and I leaned over to kiss her and said: 'You've been so good to me. I've never had such a marvellous time. Did you enjoy making love as much as I did, Diana?'

'Oh yes, it was a dreamy fuck,' she replied as I rolled off her soft body to lie beside her. 'That's the second time I've spent. Who have you fucked with before, Rupert? Did one of your horny servant girls teach you about how to pleasure a pussey? Or was it an assistant matron perhaps at St Lionel's? I've heard all about some of the goings-on in such places!'

'No, I've never ever done it before,' I confessed timidly, feeling the colour rise to my cheeks. Would the divine girl laugh at this intimate personal revelation?

But no, far from it – she clasped her hands together happily and said: 'You were a virgin and I was your first conquest? Oh, what an honour! Let me kiss your lovely cock, Rupert, he deserves every praise for his performance.' Yet even as she planted her lips upon my shaft, which now dangled flaccidly over my thighs, I realised that I still had much to learn about fucking if I wanted to become such a cocksman as the merry young men-about-town whose exploits I had read about in Clee's naughty magazine. I resolved then and there to devote my life to the study and appreciation of *l'art de faire l'amour*.

But I must return to my story – Diana and I worked on assiduously after this feast of fucking and when she showed me the result of her labours, I was most gratified to see myself immortalised through her perceptive artistry. She had sketched a most lifelike portrait of my face in bold sweeping lines, capturing the essence of my likeness and though I thought she flattered my physique (especially by the very prominent bulge under the fig leaf she was forced to paint over my cock and balls!) I told her in all candidness that for what it was worth, there could be little doubt that one day her work would hang on the walls of the Royal Academy in London.

'Do you really think so?' she said as she carefully packed up her materials and folded up her easel.

'Well, I don't suppose my words mean much to anyone but I'm going to ask you here and now to paint my picture again when I leave St Lionel's,' I said with genuine feeling.

'That's a deal – my very first commission,' she laughed. 'I won't charge you more than twenty guineas.' [*Twenty-one pounds or about thirty-five US dollars.*]

[*Diana Wigmore's later canvases, completed after her studies at the Slade School of Art, did in fact hang in the Academy's Summer Exhibitions of 1902, 1903 and 1908 and her paintings enjoyed a reasonable amount of critical and popular acclaim, especially when one of the most distinguished European connoisseurs, Count Johnny Gewirtz of Galicia, started to collect her work. Most unfortunately, many of her best pictures, which were in the Count's collection at Allendale House in Belgravia, were destroyed by enemy action during the*

31

London Blitz in 1940.

However, we will meet the attractive young artist again in Rupert's diaries for she was to be invited to join many a country-house party at the express invitation of King Edward VII. Diana first met the King at a reception given in his honour six years later in 1904 by the Lord Lieutenant of Yorkshire which was attended not only by Rupert's father, Colonel Harold Elton Fortescue Mountjoy but also by our author himself, who penned an account of the secret shenanigans that took place afterwards in the royal suite of the Grand Hotel and which will appear in a later volume of Rupert's reminiscences – Editor.]

There was ample time for us to sit on the banks of the lazily flowing nearby stream as Diana had not forgotten her self-appointed task of washing her knickers and chemise which lay drying on the sun. She had slipped on her blouse and skirt and I had also dressed myself, for though the sun still blazed down, there was the remote possibility of some hobbledehoy of a farmworker or one of Mrs Wigmore's domestics passing through the Wigmore's property on their way to work.

I threw a pebble into the water and said somewhat hesitantly to Diana. 'Don't think me nosey but when did you first, er –'

'First fuck?' she interrupted brightly, for she could see that I was still too unsophisticated to speak in vernacular terms. 'I don't mind telling you about it. Let's snuggle down together and, whilst my underwear is drying, I'll tell you all about it.

'I suppose I'd always been attracted to my brother Humphrey's best pal, Ronald Greyfriars. Ronald and Humphrey both row for Cambridge University and they spend much of their vacation time together catching up on their studies as during termtime both spend too much time on the river and not enough in the library, especially for a difficult course such as law which they were both reading at Trinity Hall. As fortune would have it, Ronald was staying with us during last year's Christmas vacation and naturally, both he and Humphrey were invited to my birthday party on December 8th. You were invited, if you remember, but had to refuse as your parents had made arrangements for you to go down to London with them on a family visit to your Uncle, the one who sits in Parliament.'

'You mean Uncle Edmund, the Liberal member for West Bristol,' I said gloomily. 'Yes, I was dashed upset at the time but my parents insisted I joined them as he thought a tour round the House of Commons would be most instructional and improve my understanding of politics. It was quite interesting but I would far, far rather have been at your party!'

'Never mind, there will be other parties – anyhow, it was only a small affair with local friends. There was no dancing but we played parlour games after dinner and I think we all enjoyed ourselves. After my guests had left, Papa and Mama went to bed and suggested that I do likewise. I did go to my room but I wasn't sleepy even though it was quite late. I looked at myself in the mirror and thought I looked rather fetching in the new dress Miss Foggin from Harrogate had made up for me. It was an evening gown in décolleté style and I insisted that it was cut as low as Mama would allow. She had insisted that it should be fringed with lace. I stepped out of the dress and took off my bodice. It was easy to unpick the fringe and when I slipped the dress back on, the cleft between my breasts was clearly visible now in the mirror when I leaned forward. I could see the swell of my breasts which were now only barely covered. The tips of my fingers passed lightly over my nipples and I thought how marvellous it would be to have Ronald's hands there in place of my own.

'As I said, I was too wide awake to sleep so I walked quietly downstairs to the library where I thought I would read the evening newspaper which I had not scanned. No-one seemed to be around although the lights were all burning, but then Armstrong rarely locks up until midnight so I was not alarmed when I thought I heard somebody moving in the drawing room. I opened the door and was pleasantly surprised to see that Ronald was still there, reading through one of his textbooks.

' "Hello Ronald, are you burning the midnight oil? It's more than Humphrey would care to do," I said.

'He rose from his chair and grinned. "Humphrey's worked harder than me or he'd be down here too to cram for these bally examinations. But golly, young Diana, you look spiffing. Wait a moment though, there's something different about you. What is it now, let me see ... By thunder, I have it, you've altered your dress. What's happened to that fringe of white lace?"

'I was not in the least embarrassed by his question and I replied: "Well, if you must know, I thought my figure was much nicer to look at than a frilly piece of material."

'He put down his book and moved closer towards me. "My God, I should say so," he said thickly. "I remember when your chest was as flat as mine." "But no more," I said, touching his arm with my hand. "I'm sixteen years old now and fully developed." His handsome face betrayed his struggle to keep his composure as I deliberately leaned forward to expose even more of my breasts to his excited gaze.

'He took a deep breath but said nothing, though I could see that this show of the snowy white globes deeply affected him. I looked steadily at his deep brown eyes and said softly: 'Why don't we sit down for a minute on the Chesterfield and talk?" [*a large tightly stuffed sofa, usually upholstered in leather, and very popular in wealthy Victorian and Edwardian homes – Editor*].

'Still without speaking, he took my hand in his own and we adjourned to the aforementioned couch. I knew full well that Ronald was simply dying to touch me but he needed some further sign of encouragement so we chatted quietly about this and that. After a while I decided that I would have to make the first move so I put my hand on his shoulder and let it rest there. This did the trick! Indeed, I had not expected him to be so forward for suddenly he spun me around, turned my face up to his and kissed me passionately on the lips.

'A surge of excitement coursed through my veins for there was something about this kiss which made it impossible for me not to respond. "Diana, you have always epitomised the very quintessence of female beauty," he muttered.

"Goodness me, that's quite a little speech,

could you not speak plainer?" I said, though I knew well enough what his convoluted words were attempting to convey.

Ronald swallowed hard and said: "I mean, my darling girl, that I have an overwhelming desire to make love to you."

"You have never mentioned this to me before," I said with a small smile, stroking his flushed cheek.

"No, because you are the sister of my best chum and in any case I would never take advantage of a girl of tender years," he replied hotly.

"Your candour does you credit," I said firmly. "However, I am not totally without experience of the joys of sensuality, though I have never actually made love yet – but now would be an appropriate time to remedy this, for as the country folk say around these parts:

When roses are reddest they're ready for plucking,
And when she's sixteen, a girl's ready for fucking!"

'Ronald smiled at my rude verse and his hand slid gently from my shoulder down underneath my arm as he positioned me to receive a further intimate embrace. Now, as our lips crushed together in a burning kiss, I felt his hand close gently over my breast. At the same time his tongue sank inside my mouth. Then I could feel his hands lift out my naked breasts from their scanty covering and he toyed with them so excitingly, tracing circles around my hardening nipples with the tips of his fingers and then rubbing them deliciously against the palms of his roving hands until they stood up in salute like small red bullets.

'But my lips could not satisfy his ardour and

soon he was passing his mouth over my cherry titties, kissing and sucking my nipples so sensually that I felt my pussey beginning to moisten. I was putty in the hands of a master builder for at this stage he leaned down to take hold of my ankle and began to caress it lovingly. I knew what was in Ronald's mind but I made no attempt to stop him as his hand worked its way up my leg and inside my thigh. A strangled cry of exultation escaped from his throat when his fingers reached inside my new pair of minute French knickers, a *sub rosa* purchase I made in Paris on my last visit to the Continent, and soon they became enmeshed with the silly hair of my pussey. Even at this stage, I was still just in control of my senses but I had no wish to end it all just yet. Ronald's fingers played exquisitely with my thatch and when he began to roll down my knickers, I assisted his efforts by raising my bum so he could more easily pull them down. Once the tiny garment was over my feet, I stepped out of them and said: "Ronnie, did you know that the hair of my bush is as blonde as the hair on my head?"

' "Nothing would give me greater pleasure than to see for myself," he panted, moaning softly as with a deliberate carelessness I let my own hand brush against the prominent vertical bulge in the lap of his trousers.

'Without further ado I unbuttoned my dress and let it slide to the floor. I stepped out of it towards him totally nude, the first time I had exposed my naked body to a man. Feeling slightly decadent, I draped myself across his clothed body on the couch, and my pussey ached with excitement as Ronald began to tear off his clothes.

His muscular frame gleamed in the light afforded by our newly installed electric lamps. His face too looked so adorable, set off by his large eyes with their thick lashes whilst their dark brown colour matched so handsomely with his tightly curled hair. But the *pièce de résistance* was of course his lovely prick which I now saw for the first time. It was exquisitely fashioned, bobbing out in front of him like a curved scimitar and his burgeoning erection had already partially pushed back the foreskin over the beautiful pink crown. All thoughts of control fled from me as I reached out and encircled his shaft with my hand, pulling down the foreskin to completely bare the full helmet of his cock which was already glistening with a blob of pre-spend that had emanated from the tiny "eye" on the tip of his knob.

'We fell back on the couch and Ronald stretched me out on the big sofa. He knelt alongside me and fervently kissed my breasts and belly – and when he placed his head lower I clutched it lovingly, moaning my approval as he pressed his lips against my silky blonde thatch. The sensations were simply divine and when I felt his tongue begin licking my pussey I almost screamed with unalloyed delight.

' "You have the most delicious cunney ever, Diana, and I could feast on it all night," he said, raising his head for a moment before carrying on his sweet sucking of my cunt. These lewd yet complimentary words raised me to an even higher pitch of excitement when he parted the lips of my love chink with his wicked fingers and started to lap between my cunney lips. He relentlessly continued this thrilling stimulation, sinking his fingers into my moistening slit, making me tremble with expectation as he eased them deeper and deeper inside my pouting pussey crack.

'His tongue and fingers were delighting me to new peaks of pleasure that I had rarely before been able to climb. My clitty was now tingling with an intense excitation as he cupped it between his lips and nibbled furiously at the erect little miniature organ of ultimate pleasure. He twisted his fingers around inside my cunney as I writhed wildly, clamping my legs around his neck, and holding his head pressed even harder against my now dripping pussey with one hand whilst the other flew from one nipple to the other, tweaking them up to attention as I felt an approaching spend begin its journey. Ronald must have sensed it too for he licked even harder at my clitty and his finger sped even faster out of my dripping slit and this fabulous pressure kept me at the highest pitch of ecstasy for what seemed to be a blissfully long time. He was a natural cunney sucker who clearly enjoyed eating pussey and I am sure that his devotion to this art – so shamefully neglected in this country although not, I am assured, by our American cousins – will always assure Ronald of an inexhaustible supply of women ready and willing to be fucked. Indeed when my climax juddered through my body, satisfying though it was, I was still more than keen to continue.

'I pulled him upwards over me and his thick stiff cock now was hovering between my thighs. But to his everlasting credit, Ronald somehow dragged himself from the point of no return and whispered: "Are you certain you want me to carry on, my darling? Say now if you want me to stop because I can scarcely hold back as it is and in a few seconds it will be too late. But if I do continue, I'll be careful not to come inside you."

' "Yes, I want you to fuck me, Ronald," I replied softly. "It will soon be my time of the month, tomorrow or probably the day after so you can shoot off in my pussey. Besides, I want to feel you come inside me."

'I laid my head back and relaxed as I watched Ronald take his cockshaft in his hand and gently insert the tip of his tool in my cunney. He pushed it in so slowly that I could feel the ridge of his cock scrape past the folds of my inner channel. Ronald felt so big inside me as my cunney muscles gripped his cock, the first penis ever to have passed through the lips of my love-channel. He pulled back almost as slowly as he had entered my virgin hole and then pushed in and out again at a slightly quicker pace.

'He looked up at me enquiringly: "I am not hurting you?" he asked anxiously. There was a slight discomfort at the very commencement of my début fuck but that very soon passed. This was doubtless due to the solitary frigging I had practised at school and perhaps too to the bouncing up and down on the saddle of my pony. Oh, do not look so shocked – do you think that only boys know how to play with themselves? But for whatever reason, I experienced no pain as Ronald's proud prick rammed in and out faster and faster and deeper and deeper inside my suppurating cavity. He now began to pump into me with great swinging thrusts as I raised my pelvis to allow him to clutch my cheeks of my pert little backside. We fucked away like a couple possessed and my body squirmed with joy as I came again and again as Ronald's cock slammed in and out of my saturated cunt. Ronald, too, was now reaching the point of no return and I could feel his prick throb inside me as his hairy ballsack banged against my thighs which were now wet with my virgin spendings of love juice and a tiny amount of blood. As he shuddered to a crashing climax, I felt a rush of liquid fire coat the back of my grotto as spasm after spasm of jism shot into my very vitals and I achieved a further spend as wave after wave of pure, unadulterated enchantment enveloped me from head to toe.

'He raised himself on his hands and knees and withdrew his cock which squelched out, still almost as stiff as when he started to fuck me, but covered now with a mix of our love juices which was tinged with the claret of my virgin emission. I must have appeared concerned for Ronald smiled and said: "Do not be concerned, the next time there will be no blood, I can promise you." He reached down to the floor and brought out a handkerchief from his trousers with which he tenderly wiped my pussey and his own cock clean. He put the handkerchief back into his pocket and said that he would treasure the ensanguined linen as a loving remembrance of how I had so gallantly surrendered my virginity to him.

' "Ah, that was a magnificent fuck. Yet I fear that all is not well for, unless I am much mistaken, I thought I noticed a frown of disappointment flicker across your face?" he asked as I turned my head slightly to one side.

' "No Ronald," I replied truthfully. "I thoroughly enjoyed making love with you. If there is any disappointment it is only because we have finished so soon and I am still feeling randy!"

' "Is that all, dearest?" he exclaimed delightedly. "Oh, but this is a situation easily rectified." He took my hand and cupped my fingers halfway round his sticky pole. "Just rub my cock up and down and watch it swell up ready to fuck you again."

'This turned out to be no idle boast for it took only a few moments of frigging before he raised himself above me and this time he let me guide his knob between the squishy lips of my infatuated pussey. Once he was settled inside my welcoming quim he needed no further urging and I eagerly lifted my hips to salute his thrusting tool. His cock was very thick and I was in heaven as he pumped his throbbing prick to and fro and he played with my breasts, tweaking my titties as they bounced back and forth, moving in perfect rhythm with the movements of his cock. My cunney was still soaking with Ronald's jism and my own love juices but it was still gloriously tight and when he increased the tempo, slamming the entire length of his shaft inside me, I thought I might expire with happiness. Oh, how the fiery currents surged through my pussey and crackled their way through every inch of my frame. In no time at all I was twisting and rolling around like a crazed animal and I shouted out: "Fuck me! Fuck me! Fuck me!" in sheer uninhibited lust.

' "Shush, shush, my precious, you'll wake up

the whole house,'' he breathed as he reamed the furthest niches of my cunney with his rampant rod. Our mouths melded together in a luscious French kiss and as we wiggled our tongues wetly in each other's mouths, he jetted his powerful emission of hot, creamy spunk just as I too reached the dazzling peaks of a truly magnificent spend.

'Well, that is the story of my first experience of the joys of love-making. As you can imagine we continued to fuck until Ronald simply had no more strength. I sucked his cock back to erection three times more that night before we crept back to our beds just as the first rays of the sun began to break through the darkness of the night sky.'

Here Diana ended her tale and after giving me a grateful nod of thanks she drank deeply from the glass of lemonade which I had poured out for her.

'Did you see him again?' I asked, wriggling around to try to accommodate my bursting cock which had naturally stiffened up to full erection whilst I listened to the stimulating story of Diana's sexual awakening.

'We did manage one more night of bliss. Alas, there were to be no other opportunities for us to indulge ourselves in any further fucking as Ronald and my brother had arranged to spend some time with Professor Aspis, one of the world's leading authorities on bats, who was staying with our friends the Grove-Radletts, who live on the Kentish coast near Herne Bay.'

'Bats?' I echoed in astonishment. 'For God's sake, what's so interesting about bats?'

'Not a great deal as far as I am concerned, but Professor Aspis is paying the boys ten pounds

43

each to assist him in catching a certain kind of bat which can only be found in caves around that area. Ronald has become quite fascinated by these little creatures, which ignorant folk think are sinister and demonic. But, as Professor Aspis has shown, they play an important part in nature and are very helpful towards us as they eat many harmful pests. In tropical climes, there are bats which feed on fruit and many trees are entirely dependent on bats to pollinate their flowers and disperse their seeds.'

'So if it weren't for the bats shifting the seeds –'

'– there would be a lack of wild species of dates, figs, guava and others,' finished Diana.

So not only had I fucked my first girl but I had also learned something of the habits of the bat – material I would make good use of when Mr Pilcher, our science teacher, set us an essay on a subject of our choosing. But my thoughts were still centred around matters connected with human biology – namely, whether the beautiful Diana would allow me to fuck her again before we parted. I even made so bold as to ask but she shook her pretty head and said: 'No Rupert, I really don't have the time. But meet me tomorrow afternoon around half past two in the old barn next to our stables and we can enjoy ourselves again there.'

Her reply brought a gleam of pleasure to my eyes but suddenly my face fell – tomorrow morning I would be playing host to my chum Frank Folkestone. 'Drat it!' I exclaimed as I spelt out my predicament to Diana. 'No, don't worry yourself – bring Frank along and I'll ask my friend Cecily Cardew to join us,' she cried. 'We'll have some real larks, I promise you, if your friend can show her a good-sized stiffstander.'

My heart leaped with joy. 'I'll say he can – Frank's prick is the biggest in our dormitory. When he gets a hard-on his shaft rises so high that the tip is on the same level as his belly button.'

'That's something Cecily and I will really look forward to seeing – goodbye, Rupert, and thanks again for posing so patiently. When I've finished all my work, I'll frame my study of your body and give it to you for Christmas. See you tomorrow in the old barn.'

We kissed each other fondly on the cheek and I walked home briskly to arrive just in time for tea.

CHAPTER TWO

A Whoresome Foursome

THE SUNLIGHT WAS ALREADY BEAMING THROUGH MY BEDROOM curtains when I awoke early the next morning. As usual, my sturdy young penis was as hard as a brick and, as was my regular habit, I gripped my smooth shaft in my right hand, frigging it slowly up and down as I closed my eyes and dreamed with lustful anticipation of what might be in store for me that afternoon. The previous evening I had tossed myself off twice thinking about how Diana Wigmore had sucked my cock and then later had allowed me to fuck her. It occured to me that I should not spend this morning if I wanted to perform properly in the afternoon. But there was no way I could resist rubbing my prick in my closed fist until I had spent copiously all over my pyjamas. In my haste I had forgotten to reach out for the spunk-stained handkerchief I kept hidden in my bedside drawer! I have always enjoyed a good wank and take issue with those foolish folk who warn against the practice for supposed reasons of health or morality. On this occasion, though, after the riches of genuine fucking, the joys of self-induced simulation were but limited. I cursed silently as I leapt out of bed and unknotted the cord of my pyjama trousers. I put them in my laundry basket and hoped that the sticky stain would be undetected by the servants before the offending garment was washed.

I looked at my watch. As it was only just after six-thirty, I decided to polish up some verses I had composed when I returned home after my fateful meeting with Diana. I sat at my desk and, after poring over an exercise book, pronounced myself satisfied with the following poem of praise to my new-found love:

> Oh when I shall behold, my love,
>   Your merry eyes, your fair-skinned
>   face
> I cannot wait until my arms
>   Enclose you in my tight embrace.
>
> Yet though I've sworn so many times
>   The world no sight can show,
> To match your locks, your lips divine,
>   Your bosoms' hills of snow.
>
> For sweeter now is what I have seen,
>   Two lips have I beheld
> And lovelier on a happy day,
>   A mound which does excel.
>
> Your breasts can boast no swell as fair,
>   No teats that these eclipse;
> Your lovely face can scarce compete
>   With such enchanting lips.

> For now I've seen your hairy mount
> Where all your favours centre,
> Yes! I have fucked your juicy cunt
> And wish again to enter!

'Well, it might not stand up to a Shakespearean sonnet, but then neither should it be thrown back in my face,' I muttered to myself as I then jotted down the draft of a covering letter:

Dearest Diana,

I dedicate these verses to you – I can think of no better way to express my heartfelt love and gratitude for the way you initiated me into the joys of coition. I will never forget our glorious love-making as long as I live.

Your ever affectionate friend,

Rupert

I put the exercise book safely away (or so I thought at the time!) in my bedside drawer, resolving to copy out the poem carefully in my best writing and give it to Diana with a bunch of flowers which I could obtain from Stamford, our ancient head gardener, who had been employed at Albion Hall for the last thirty-five years. I then ran a refreshing cool bath. Doubtless because I could not clear my mind of the promised joys to come, my prick refused to lie down until my soapy face flannel had travelled up and down the shaft to provide the necessary manual relief.

My father had already taken an early breakfast and left the house when I arrived downstairs, for the local petty sessions began today and he had sat on the bench as a senior magistrate since the family had returned home from India. My mother was also preparing to leave as she had a committee meeting of the Liberal Association to attend that morning. (Much to my father's chagrin, I should add, for he was a crusty old Tory. To his credit, though, it must be added that he simply accepted the fact that Mama and later myself were both wedded to a progressive political philosophy, even when we both staunchly supported the Suffragette Movement which demanded the right of women to vote.)

'Would you please pass my apologies to Frank, dear, as I doubt if I shall be here to greet him when he arrives,' said my Mama as she passed me the morning newspaper. 'This meeting will probably drag on until mid-afternoon as we have to choose our candidates for the forthcoming county council elections and for some reason there are more budding politicians than ever. Now your Papa has commandeered the motor car to drive to court and I shall need the Brougham [*a large four-wheeled carriage – Editor*] so I suggest you go with Wallace in the landaulet to the station and meet your friend there. His train arrives at Ripley Valley station just before a quarter past eleven. Remember to leave in good time as it's market day and the roads are likely to be congested.'

If anything, it was even warmer than the previous day and I closed the folding hood over the passenger compartment as Wallace, our second coachman, drove at a steady pace through Ripley, a pretty village whose main street is prettily shaded with trees. Its fifteenth century church has marks on the outside of the east wall that are attributed to bullets fired by Cromwell's soldiers – some say, when shooting prisoners taken at Marston Moor during the English Civil War. I made a mental note to take Frank on a walking trip round these parts as history is his favourite subject and he would be fascinated to see the house in the village of Scotton where Guy Fawkes lived as a young man.

We arrived ten minutes before Frank's train was due so Wallace and I sat sunning ourselves on the platform whilst we waited for the train. It arrived punctually and Frank jumped out eagerly to greet me. 'Hullo, Rupert, how smashing to see you,' he said, heartily shaking my hand. 'My mother gated me until I was over this poxy chill but I'm fighting fit now and ready for anything. I know that you're not that keen on cricket but tennis is all the rage in town these days. I've brought up a couple of rackets and some balls so we could have a game – it'll be great fun especially in this weather. Your neighbour, Doctor Wigmore, laid out a court if I remember rightly – if you haven't fallen out with him perhaps he would let us play on it.'

I grinned as Wallace collected Frank's cases and we walked over to the exit. 'I haven't seen Doctor Wigmore since the Easter vacation but I met his daughter Diana yesterday,' I said with a grin.

'Fine, perhaps she would also be keen to play? How about this afternoon if the weather stays fine?'

I was sorely tempted to reply: 'I'll say, but at a much better game than tennis!' But I held my tongue until we were seated in the coach and Wallace had driven us out of the station yard.

Once we were on our way I turned to him and said: 'Frank, I like playing tennis and though you'll probably beat me hollow I'll do my best to give you some sort of a game. But I've already made other plans for us this afternoon which, as it happens, involve Diana and one of her girl friends.'

'Well, that's all right, we could play doubles.'

I gestured impatiently. 'Listen, old boy, forget tennis for a moment. How would you like to play a game you've dreamed about since you've had hair growing round your cock?' As I expected, this startled him into an astonished silence! 'You heard,' I repeated. 'I'm not joking, no really I wouldn't jape about something so important. Just play your cards right, young Folkestone, and you'll be fucking a pretty girl this afternoon just like I did yesterday! It beats tossing off any day of the week, I can tell you!'

'I don't believe it, Rupert, you're having me on, aren't you?' he said, half-afraid perhaps to accept such wonderful news and then be brought down to earth with a hefty bump when he learned that I was only teasing him.

'Honestly, I'm not joshing, Frank, I swear I'm not,' I earnestly assured my pal. I went on to tell him of my great adventure into manhood and how Diana and her friend Cecily would meet us at the old barn that very afternoon for some further frolics.

'This sounds too good to be true,' he breathed. 'Why, the very thought is already making me feel terribly randy!' He wriggled uncomfortably in his seat and I could clearly see the bulge in his lap.

'Ha! Ha! Ha! That's made you forget all about

tennis, hasn't it?' I laughed. 'Well, Diana wanted to know if you were ready for your first fuck and, from the size of your stiffstander, I don't think she and Cecily will be too disappointed!'

'They won't be disappointed at all,' he said with mock indignation. 'Haven't I got the thickest prick in our dormitory? Look, I'll show you, I bet you can't match this for size!' He ripped open his fly buttons, releasing his big red-headed cock, which stood up stiffly as he frigged it up to its fullest measure.

He then helped me pull out my own stiff truncheon which, though not so massive an instrument, was still substantial enough to have satisfied Diana Windsor – as I hastened to remind him. We were now so fired up that we handled each other's tools in an ecstacy of anticipatory delight, and the proceeding ended by a mutual tossing off, aiming each other's emissions of gluey white jism onto the newspaper which luckily I had brought with me to read on the way to the station.

'Well, I hope no-one wants to read *The Times* any more today,' I quipped as we entered our carriage drive. 'I'll hide it in my jacket and chuck it in a bin when we get indoors and if anybody asks for the paper, I'll say I left it on the platform by mistake whilst helping you down with your luggage.'

Goldhill, the new butler Mama had persuaded to our household from Lord Mozer's establishment, was ready to greet us at the front door. As instructed I dutifully passed on Mama's message to Frank and Goldhill asked me at what time Mrs Randall should serve luncheon. 'Oh, one o'clock will suit well enough, only do tell her that we will require only a very light meal – I would suggest perhaps one of her famous cheese omelettes with fried potatoes and a green salad with a fruit *compote* to follow.

'Would that suit you?' I asked, turning to Frank. 'Absolutely spot-on,' he replied with a grin. 'We don't want too much to eat if we're going to take some strenuous exercise this afternoon.'

Goldhill nodded. 'Very good, Master Rupert. Might you young gentlemen be playing tennis later, for I noticed that Master Frank has brought his tennis rackets. Your equipment is in the games room and I'll get one of the maids to bring it downstairs for you. Will you also require balls?' With a great effort my chum stifled his laughter as I gravely replied: 'Yes, we'll need our balls this afternoon, Goldhill. But I'll help you unpack, Frank, and we can take our tennis togs with us in my games bag.'

Now as you may imagine, dear reader, Frank and I hardly did justice to Mrs Randall's tasty fare. We bolted through our luncheon and stuffed our tennis clothes – white short-sleeved shirts and thin white cotton trousers – into two sports bags. 'Pack all your stuff in one of your own cases, Frank. I've just remembered a couple of things to take that we'll find very useful.'

We were in so much of a hurry that Goldhill had to remind us to take our rackets! 'You won't play very much tennis without these, young gentlemen,' said the old retainer with a grave smile. 'With luck we won't be playing with them at all!' muttered Frank under his breath.

When we were on our way down the drive he turned to me and said: 'Rupert, I don't doubt your sworn word but I'm still frightened that this is all a lovely dream and that in a minute I'll wake up in bed with an aching stiff prick!'

'Have no fear, the girls will not let us down,' I reassured him, although I too could hardly take in our good fortune. We reached the old barn ten minutes before the appointed hour and I spread out on the clean wooden floor the eiderdown I had packed in my bag. '*Voilà*, this should make for more comfortable fucking,' I said with satisfaction.

'Yes, so long as the girls arrive,' said Frank, nervously moving his weight from one foot to the other.

'Why don't we change into our tennis outfits?' I suggested. 'It will help pass the time and we won't have so many clothes to take off when we begin our fun.'

'What a good idea,' he agreed and we took off our shoes and socks and then our trousers, taking care to fold them neatly before placing them in our valises.

We had both just taken off our shirts and were standing solely in our drawers when the door opened and the forms of our two frisky young fillies stood framed in the sunlight. Never before nor ever since have I clapped eyes on two such superb contrasting examples of female pulchritude. The blonde beauty of Diana was marvellously complemented by the equally pretty Cecily's wavy brown hair, her graceful Grecian face of rosy cheeks, large dark eyes and lips as rich and red as midsummer cherries. The exquisite girl was deliciously proportioned with large, heavy breasts covered only by a cream-coloured blouse, of such fine silk that it was almost transparent. Frank and I could easily make out the shadow of her swollen nipples that pressed so invitingly against the softness of her clothing.

'Goodness me, were you two boys planning to begin the proceedings without us?' said Diana brightly. 'Cecily, I do hope that these two boys have not been seduced into the ways of Oscar Wilde and the homosexualists!'

The other girl chuckled, showing pearly white teeth which we were to see frequently exhibited in a later succession of winning smiles that were rarely to leave her charming face. 'It would mean that we will have wasted our afternoon, but they might just be changing their clothes to prepare themselves for our visit.'

'Indeed, that this precisely what we were doing,' I grinned back. 'Frank, I have the honour to introduce Miss Diana Wigmore. Miss Wigmore, this is Frank Folkestone, my best friend at St Lionel's.'

'How do you do?' said Frank, shaking hands with the cool blonde beauty.

'Very well thank you – what a funny experience being introduced to a boy unclothed except for his drawers! Still, I will give you both the benefit of the doubt as to why you are both so scantily clad and introduce my best friend, Miss Cecily Cardew of Harrogate. Mr Folkestone, Mr Rupert Mountjoy, Miss Cardew.'

The formalities over, I asked the girls if they would care for some refreshment. I flourished an ice-box in which stood a bottle of champagne that

I had sneaked out of our cellar before luncheon. 'There are even four glasses inside it,' I explained as I opened it up. 'My Uncle Gilbert gave it to me for Christmas last year, isn't it a useful gift?'

We rapidly finished off the bottle of Krug '87 and, though we were far from being blotto, the bubbly fizz certainly loosened our tongues. We were very soon engaged in a most relaxed and friendly conversation. Earlier in the morning Diana had also brought a quilt into our secret hide-out on which she and I sat, whilst Frank and Cecily lolled together on the duvet I had taken from one of our spare bedrooms.

'We had a good fuck yesterday, didn't we, Rupert?' said Diana chattily.

'It wasn't good, it was magnificent!' I responded, putting my arm around her waist. 'I can't wait to fuck you again.'

'All in good time, you randy boy, all in good time,' she riposted. 'But what I really would like first is to see Frank fuck Cecily – we have presumed that, like Rupert, Frank has never before made love and Cecily has a great urge to rectify this sad situation. Haven't you, my dearest? Despite being only seventeen years old, she is far more experienced than I, having tasted the fleshpots of London with Sir David Nash and all the other young rogues of Belgravia.'

'Not *all* of the others, if you please, Diana, though I could tell you a tale or two about Lord Andrew Stuck and his friend Matthew Cosgrave! Still, I will admit, dear Frank, that the idea of fucking your virgin prick very much appeals to me. In fact, I have quite a fancy for it right now. How do you feel about the matter?'

Frank gulped and said: 'I'd like nothing better'. But we could see that he was nervous and I knew how he must be feeling – I too had butterflies in my tummy just before I made love to Diana, and that was without any spectators to witness the event!

'Go on, Frank, don't mind us,' I said to try and help my friend. 'We're going to kiss and cuddle as well, don't you know.'

Cecily stood up and let her tongue pass sensuously over her lips as she slowly unhooked the tiny buttons of her blouse. With feline grace she opened the garment to reveal the luscious swell of her large breasts topped by nut-brown nipples, already as hard as little sticks, sticking out at least a whole inch in length. She cupped these exciting globes in her hands and, kneeling down in front of Frank, she rubbed the palm of her hand against the bulging erection hidden in his drawers.

'Dear me, Frank, it was just as well you began to undress before Diana and I arrived – I do so hate wasting time with unnecessary preliminaries. Now, is that a cucumber you have hidden in your pants or are you really excited by my bare titties?' she asked with a mischievous glint in her sparkling brown eyes. Alas, poor Frank was so overcome by his emotions that, though at school he was rarely lost for words, the thrilling sight of this exquisite half-naked girl left him completely tongue-tied and he could not find his voice to make a reply to this amusingly rhetorical question. Indeed, the poor chap was so overwhelmed that he made no attempt to help Cecily when she took hold of his undershorts and tried to tug them down.

'Frank, old fellow, lift yourself up,' I urged. This did the trick, for he recovered his composure and

raised his arse so that Cecily could slide his
drawers under his bum. She then lifted them over
his stalwart staff which was standing as high as a
flagpole. Diana craned her head forward for a
closer look at his tremendous erection – for it was
no idle boast that Frank had made earlier on our
way home from the station when he laid claim to
be the proud owner of the thickest prick in the
Upper Fourth form at St Lionel's – and the two
girls admired the tumescent proportions of
Frank's cock. 'What a whopper for such a young
sport!' cried Cecily, stroking Frank's throbbing
tadger with the tips of her fingers. 'It *is* one of the
biggest I've ever seen,' agreed Diana. 'My sweet
Cecily, I wonder if you will be able to
accommodate such a monster.'

'Just watch me,' Cecily advised her friend. 'I
have not yet come up against a prick that is
too big for me to suck.' Both Diana and I admired
her dextrous technique as she began by clasping
Frank's plump penis with both of her small
hands, and massaging his gigantic tool up to
bursting point. She then leaned over and took the
mushroomed head of the purple bulb between
her lips, jamming down his foreskin and lashing
her tongue around the rigid shaft. She tickled his
helmet with the tip of her pink little tongue and
then she opened her mouth to take in almost half
his enormous erection whilst her hands played
with his hairy ballsack. She swallowed hard and
then somehow managed to take in almost all of
his swollen stem. Diana and I watched in
fascination as her tongue flicked out to lick the
soft underfolds of skin along the base of Frank's
shaft. She sucked lustily upon his succulent cock,

sliding her lips along the rock-hard rod, gulping noisily as the helmet of his smooth skinned knob slid against the roof of her mouth to the back of her throat.

'He'll spunk too soon if she's not very careful,' Diana whispered to me as her hand slipped inside my under-shorts to grasp my own pulsing organ, which had already ballooned up to stand stiffly upwards. The soft touch of Diana's fingers soon set my tool twitching with excitement.

Cecily had also surmised this probability and she pulled her head up and said to Frank: 'Here it comes, Frank – your very first fuck. Lie down on your back and let me take charge.' He did not have to be asked a second time as he lay back, his thick prick poking up in salute as she swiftly pulled off her skirt. My cock throbbed uncontrollably at the sight of the curly brown bush that surrounded the visible lips of her pussey cunney lips! Now totally nude, Cecily straddled Frank and took hold of his yearning tool and placed it at the gateway of her cunt. 'Ready, steady, go!' she cried as she slid down his cock until it was totally engulfed in the warm, wet walls of her cunney. As soon as it was lodged deep inside, she swayed back and forth. Frank frantically arched his body up and down and his face reddened and his breathing quickened until, as we expected, he shot his sperm right up inside her.

Cecily raised herself off Frank's prick which now glistened with their liquid libations. She grasped hold of his sperm-coated shaft, which was still almost as stiff as when she had first sat on it, and after a few quick wanks, his cock was back up to its full majestic height. 'Now it's your turn to call the tune!' she said gaily as she lay down and pulled his sinewy body over her. Frank's shaft slid joyously into her hungry pussey and, with barely a pause to take breath, he started to pump up and down in a steady rhythm, his arse quivering with every movement of his hips.

Looking back on this erotic event, I must say that although this was his first fuck, Frank had a natural understanding of what was required of him. He did not rush in and out like a man possessed – perhaps because Cecily had cleverly decided to get his first spunking out of the way as quickly as possible – but he thrust home steadily, taking his time as he withdrew and then re-entered the juicy haven of her cunt. This pleased Cecily, who began to toss and turn as she gasped: 'Oh, lovely, really lovely, Frank, you big-cocked boy – ram in harder, you won't hurt me! Ah! That's the ticket! I want to spend as well, you know!'

Her bottom ground and rolled violently as she threshed madly under his renewed onslaught. She clawed Frank's back and he grasped her shoulders and began to ride her like a cowboy on a bucking bronco. Her legs slid down, her heels drumming a tattoo on the quilt as she arched her body upwards, working her cunney back and forth to meet the fierce thrusts of Frank's powerful tool.

'I'm coming, yes, I'm coming! Yes, there I go!' screamed Cecily as Frank shuddered, his penis sheathed so fully inside her cunt that his balls nestled against the luscious cheeks of her bum. With one last mighty shove in and out of her pulsating pussey, he sent the trembling girl right off into the sweet ecstasies of a superb spend as his prick squirted jets of glutinous white sperm exploding inside her cunney, on and on until the last dribblings oozed out and he sank down on top of her, his weight pinning her to the ground as the last delicious throbs died away. Cecily manoeuvred him to her side and they lay together in each other's arms, panting heavily to get back their breath, but with blissful smiles of fulfilment upon their faces as they sensibly let their exhausted bodies enjoy a well deserved rest.

This first-rate fucking had so galvanised both Diana and myself that her hand travelled faster and faster up and down my own hard stiffstander and almost immediately after Frank had shot his load, my own trusty tool also sent a fountain of spunk high into the air and I spent copiously, sending blobs of jism over the sleeve of Diana's dress!

I apologised profusely, saying with some embarrassment: 'Oh dear, I am so sorry, that's the second time I've spent over your clothes.'

But Diana refused to blame me and said: 'No, please don't apologise, the fault was all mine. I should have taken off my clothes before I started to toss you off. Let's both undress now – I far prefer to fuck naked anyway and we won't have to worry about any further accidents.'

We stood up and I pulled down my pants as Diana threw her dress over her head to reveal that the naughty girl had already dispensed with her underclothes. Her beautiful bare breasts, with their jutting red nipples and the abundant thatch of silky blonde hair between her legs fired me with the most urgent desire. My penis gradually swelled up to its former height and hardness and suddenly her tousled blonde hair was between my legs as she kissed my now rampant cock. Her tongue flicked out and washed my unhooded helmet and when she opened the lips wide and encircled my staff, instinctively I moved forward to push my prick even further inside her mouth. Her wicked tongue lapped all over my knob, savouring the blob of juice which had already formed around the top, and her teeth scraped the tender flesh as she drew me in between her luscious lips, sucking in all of my shaft and sending shivers of pure pleasure racing from my thrilled tool throughout my entire body. She circled the base with her hand and started to bob her head in the most sensual of rhythms as she sucked away with gusto. Then she let my cock fall from her mouth to nibble and slurp her tongue upon the soft wrinkled skin of my ballsack. This sent me into fresh paroxyms of delight. Finally, she filled her mouth with saliva and again palated my prick as I plunged my raging shaft between her lips. Very shortly afterwards I let out a great bellow and spent copiously, filling her mouth with the hot gush of sperm that cascaded out of my throbbing tool. She gulped down my spend with obvious enjoyment, drinking me dry as slowly but inevitably my sated shaft shrank down to dangle down flaccidly between my thighs.

Diana led me back to our eiderdown and I sank down, quite *hors de combat* after this strenuous erotic engagement. Diana stood over me and sighed: 'Oh Rupert, your poor little cockie looks so forlorn. I suppose it needs a rest.'

I nodded dumbly as Cecily called out: 'I'm

afraid that I have the same problem with Frank's cock, Di – look, it just flops around all over the place.' And to prove her point, she took hold of his limp penis and rested it in the palm of her hand. She squeezed his shaft and rolled back his foreskin to uncover his knob, but his recalcitrant rammer stayed obstinately in a deflated state.

'Please, just give us a little more time to recover,' Frank begged with heartfelt vehemence. Cecily cocked her head to one side and then snapped her fingers as a new plan of action suggested itself to her. 'I have just thought of the solution to all our problems,' she exclaimed, rising to her feet. 'Frank, you go over there and sit down with Rupert. Diana, you come and lie down here and we will show the boys how well we can manage without their silly pricks.' Now remember, friendly reader, that Frank and I were the merest novices in *l'art de faire l'amour*, so do not be surprised when I say that whilst we readily obeyed Cecily's request, we truly had no real inkling of what was in her lewd mind.

Frank scrambled to his feet and came across to join me. Meanwhile, to our amazement, Diana had taken his place in Cecily's arms. They kissed like sisters at first, their lips meeting in a tentative brushing that gradually deepened into a firmer urgency. Then their mouths opened and Cecily slid her hands up and down Diana's back until the blonde beauty was shuddering in her arms, thrusting her breasts and pussey forward as her own hands slid down to squeeze the plump cheeks of Cecily's dimpled bottom. The two young women were now kissing and cuddling with great affection, and Frank and I watched in astonishment as they ran their hands around each other's breasts and thighs, squealing with delight. Cecily pushed Diana backwards and began to tongue her ear with rapid little flicks of her tongue. This brought moans of joy from the blonde girl who squeezed her legs together and murmured her encouragement as Cecily pressed her long nipples between her fingers before substituting her tongue, drawing circles all around Diana's titties before dipping her head downwards over her white belly towards her golden fluffy nest. She kissed all around Diana's honey-coloured bush before she separated her folds with her fingers to coax out the first dribbles of love juice from her pretty pussey. Diana opened her legs even further apart and all three of us could see the red crack of her cunt.

'Oooh, I'm so wet, get your fingers in me quickly!' she pleaded. Cecily immediately obliged, inserting one, then two fingers inside her squelchy cunney, rubbing and playing with the gaping crimson slit, working her fingers in and out slowly at first and then faster and faster as Diana's cunney became wetter and wetter. She found the stiff button of her clitty and frigged it by twiddling the little rosebud with her thumb and forefinger whilst with the other hand she played with Diana's nipples, rubbing them against her palm which made Diana shriek with delight as she spent all over Cecily's questing fingers.

'Now it's my turn to repay the compliment,' said Diana when she had recovered her composure. 'My pussey is more than ready to receive you,' replied Cecily, stretching out languidly like a spoiled contented kitten. Diana pulled herself on top of the dark-haired girl, positioning herself so that their pussey mounds ground together and then she leaned forward first to nibble Cecily's chewy, rubbery nipples and then working her mouth all over her gorgeous breasts, her flat white belly and inexorably downwards to her curly brown muff. Cecily had clipped her bush around her cunney lips and the pressure of Diana's lips around there was very soon sending her wild.

Now at the beginning of this two-girl exhibition, the sight of the two tribades making love to each other had filled Frank and myself with a new surging lust. By this stage in the proceedings both our pricks had risen up to a vigorous erectness.

'By Gad, I'd give anything to be there with them,' I murmured as I smoothed the tips of my fingers along the smooth underside of my knob.

'Do you think they'd mind?' Frank muttered, his hand now also gripped around his thick cock, capping and uncapping his swollen helmet which bulged over his clenched fist.

'Well, I suppose we ought to wait for an invitation, though I'm sure they would not be offended if we asked. Let Diana finish sucking Cecily's pussey and then I'll say something.'

Not long afterwards, my judgement was vindicated by the lewd girls, both of whom very much enjoyed playing with each other as an occasional change – for as Cecily was later to remark, as in most all other activities, variety is the spice of life – but their main preference was for throbbing stiff pricks in their cunnies.

We did not have to sit on the sidelines long, for Diana was soon hard at work – though work is hardly the correct word for she kissed Cecily's large nipples before saying: 'What a pretty girl you are, darling! Such firm, proud breasts and as for your pretty pussey, just looking at those pouting lips and the red crack between them makes my own cunney wet! If only I were a man, I would like nothing better than to stick my big hard cock in your cunt and spend all day pleasuring your pouting pussey. Damn, I don't even have a dildo here to push in and out of your slit! Never mind though, let's see if I can bring you off with my tongue. After all, I haven't failed to do it yet, have I?'

When she ascertained that Cecily's cunney was ready for the attack, she grasped the quivering girl's bum cheeks, one in each hand, and gently kissed Cecily's dampening slit, her mouth probing against the yielding fleshy lips, nuzzling her face against the curly brown hairs of Cecily's love-mound. She rubbed the brunette's heavy breasts, making the titties stand out like two dark little bullets, as she softly repeated her rude plan of action to make Cecily spend, about how she was going to slip her tongue into Cecily's cunt and rub her mouth all around it as she sucked her clitty.

These lewd musings fired Cecily's fancy and she cried 'Do it, yes, do it!' as Diana plunged her face into her muff and passed her tongue lasciviously around the cunney lips. Cecily yelped as the clever minx found her clitty almost at once and began teasing the erect little rubbery flesh which now projected out from Cecily's crack.

'Oh Diana, you are the best cunney sucker in the world!' she screamed, her legs now drumming against the ground as the other girl continued to work her face into the sopping cleft between her thighs. Diana sucked harder and harder with increasing ardour, rolling her tongue round and round, lapping up the aromatic love juices which were now freely flowing from Cecily's cunney. Within less than a minute, this relentless stimulation achieved its desired effect as Cecily cried: 'Oooh! Aaaah! A–h–r–e! Yes, I'm there, I'm there!' She started to spend as her hips bucked, her back rippled and then with a final little scream her cunney spurted its final tribute, splattering Diana's face and filling her mouth with the tangy essence which she greedily lapped up. Cecily shuddered into limpness as her delicious crisis slowly melted away.

By now, Frank and I could scarcely contain ourselves and it was with great joy that we heard Diana call out: 'Come on, you two – your cocks should be rock-hard by now.' Indeed they were, and in a trice we were at their side. 'Lie down beside me, Frank,' ordered Diana who immediately clamped her red lips around Frank's prick and began sucking it with unashamed relish. Cecily then heaved herself up and told me to also kneel down. She encircled her hands around my throbbing staff and began to play with it, hugging it and pressing it against her gorgeous big breasts, squeezing it between them, pressing it against her cheeks, gently rubbing it with her hands and taking my bared helmet between her rich, full lips, softly tantalising it with her wet little tongue. She now sucked on my truncheon in earnest, lashing her tongue around my pulsating pole, and drawing my shaft inside her hot, wet mouth.

The sensation was unbelievably grand but a short throaty cry from Frank made me turn my head to one side, just in time to see him spend. Diana was fucking his huge cock so voluptuously with her mouth that he could no longer delay his spend. He shot off his spunk with a final thrust as she milked his agitated penis of sperm, noisily emptying his tightly scrunched-up balls and gulping down his copious emission of sticky white jism as his twitching tool slid forwards and backwards between her lips.

An apprehensive whimper escaped my lips as Cecily decided to pull back her mouth from my own palpitating prick and substituted her hand which was tightly grasped around the base of my shaft. 'Oh, please don't stop sucking, Cecily, it was so delicious. I was just about to come in your mouth!' I pleaded unsuccessfully, for she had hauled herself up to sit pressed against me.

'Never mind, darling, instead just look at Diana, the saucy minx – don't you agree that she possesses the most succulent backside you could ever wish to see! Doesn't the brazen hussey enjoy showing it off! Well now, so far you've fucked her juicy cunney, Rupert, and in return she has sucked your sturdy stiff prick. Now perhaps you are ready to perform a further service for her.' She breathed sensuously in my ear and, as Frank sank back on his haunches, Diana wriggled her body around to present me with a full view of her rounded bum cheeks. Cecily continued her lewd whispering: 'Now feast your eyes on the lovely globes of her bottom, Rupert, and just think of how exciting it would be to slew your thick prick between those luscious beauties she is flaunting shamelessly in front of you?'

These lewd thoughts fired my imagination but still I hesitated. 'Perhaps so,' I questioned. 'But how can you be so certain that Diana would like me to do what you propose?'

'Ask her yourself if you must, but I know well enough what she wants,' replied Cecily, nipping my ear-lobe with her sharp little teeth. But I had no need to take this matter further for Diana turned her head round and looked up to us. She suggestively thrust her pert bottom upwards and said, smilingly: 'She is right, Rupert, I really would enjoy having your cock up my arse! But first, dear Cecily, would you be kind enough to anoint Rupert's penis with the pomade [*a popular perfumed hair oil of the era – Editor*] you will find in my bag? He has such a thick shaft that it will need the extra lubrication.'

'Of course, Diana, it will give me the greatest pleasure to smear the pomade upon his sturdy stiffstander,' cried Cecily, rising to perform the errand demanded by her lovely friend. She rummaged through Diana's bag and triumphantly brought out the bottle of oil. She slicked a liberal amount upon my throbbing cock so sweetly that my cock threatened to release a libation of spunk before even beginning its planned libidinous journey between Diana's quivering buttocks.

To prevent such a dreadfully unfortunate occurrence, I gritted my teeth and somehow cast my mind to a subject so tedious that it would send the sperm reversing back along its channel to my balls. So I concentrated upon the conjugation of the dullest irregular Latin verb to prevent myself sending a gush of jism all over her hand. By this titanic effort, I managed to hold back the flow of semen that had already been manufactured in my balls. I must mention, incidentally, that I have used this stratagem ever since. Without a shadow of doubt it has benefitted my command of the majestic language of ancient Rome and – which is of far more importance – has indubitably heightened my ability to hold back flooding my partner's pussey until she too is ready to release the tangy liquid elixir of her own spend.

However, on this occasion, Diana leaned forward to raise even higher the chubby white cheeks of her arse. Cecily carefully positioned my knob between them. 'Push forward slowly but firmly,' advised Cecily, realising that I was new to the sport of bum-fucking. I parted Diana's buttocks to open up her wrinkled little bum-hole that beckoned me in so invitingly. Then I followed Cecily's advice and pushed forward steadily as instructed. Despite my worry that I might injure dear Diana, I was able to shove forward without any problem until my prick was completely ensheathed in her bottom, with my balls touching the backs of her inner thighs. I rested a moment and then slowly began to pull my penis backwards and forwards. It was obvious from the high-pitched little yelps from Diana and the wriggling of her delicious arse that she was enjoying it as much as I was, and she grabbed my hands and took them to her front saying: 'Wrap your arms around my waist and frig my cunt.' This I was naturally more than happy to do. Her cunney expelled a veritable little rivulet of love juice as I twiddled her clitty and the tingling contractions of her rear dimple soon brought a torrential discharge of jism crashing out from my cock into her back passage.

'Oh yes, yes, what a lovely big spend, my God! Frig my clitty, Rupert, I'm coming too! Aaah! What lus – lus – luscious pleasure!' She almost fainted away as, with last maddened writhe, she spent copiously all over my hand as I furiously pumped out the final milky drains of sperm into her bottom.

'My God, look everybody, my prick's ready again!' called out young Frank, stroking the swollen shaft which stood up proudly between his legs.

'Well, don't let's waste it,' cried Cecily. 'Let's have some action rather than mere words!'

This spurred Frank to cover her mouth with a burning kiss and the randy girl responded by reaching out for his stiffened staff, holding it firmly between her long, tapering fingers.

Gad! At this tender age we could fuck like fury and still have stiff cocks after several spends. As my friend (for I had the privilege of meeting the great writer on many occasions and I refuse to condemn his artistic works simply because the chap was a sexual deviant) Oscar Wilde has said: 'Youth is wasted upon the young.' [*Most modern readers would applaud Rupert's staunch defence of Wilde, himself a former Cremornite and the author of such classic plays as* The Importance Of Being Earnest. *He was shunned by the vast majority of people after being jailed for homosexual offences yet was lionised by Society before the scandal broke out – Editor*]

Cecily groaned with pleasure as Frank slid his hand between her legs, running his fingers

71

through her hairy mound and, as they rolled together on the eiderdown, he opened her tender cunney lips, sliding his fingers into that dainty crack that was already moistening to a squelchy wetness. He continued to frig her with one, two and then three fingers as she took hold of his throbbing tool with both hands. Wriggling herself across him, she bent her face forward to receive the bared purple domed knob between her eager lips. She sucked at the mushroom helmet, her soft tongue rolling over and over it as she slipped her hands underneath to cup his tight hairy ballsack. She palated his pulsating prick for a little longer before rolling on to her back, her eyes closed, her mouth open.

She was ready to be fucked and Frank was more than ready to oblige. He positioned himself on top of her, balancing his weight upon the palms of his hands as Cecily took hold of his straining cock and placed it between her yearning cunney lips that opened like magic to receive it. 'Let me have it all!' urged Cecily as Frank thrust forward, burying his penis deep inside her willing love channel. She wrapped her legs around his waist as she bucked vigorously, her buttocks coming off the soft quilt as she gyrated from side to side. She began to moan, her breathing increasing to short, sharp pants as Frank's pounding quickened to a crescendo and then the surging cries of fulfilment burst forth from their throats as they began to orgasm together, with Cecily milking Frank's thick cock which was pistoning in and out of her sopping cunt. 'Keep going! Keep going!' she screamed as she arched her hips to welcome the approaching spend and happily Frank was able to continue to squirt his spermy white tribute inside her as she shuddered to a wonderful climax.

The young couple sank back exhausted into the happy reverie that follows the opening of the gates of love and my own cock was now standing as stiff as a poker as Diana stood in front of me with a pensive look in her eyes. We kissed and as our bodies crushed together she slid her hand down to my backside and without warning slipped a finger into my arse-hole. I gasped with the shock and my shaft responded by butting forward blindly against her silky blonde muff. She released her finger from between my clenched buttocks and guided my cock to her pouting cunney lips. An exquisite sensation spread over my shaft as the hairy dryness of her bush gave way to the damp promise of her wet cunt.

Rubbing herself up against me, she continued to urge my bursting knob inside her ever-opening crack. Then, with the easy grace of a ballet dancer, she lifted her right leg and hooked it around my waist. At once my member slid at least halfway inside her cunt and, as I pressed myself deeper inside her salivating cunney, she carefully linked her hands behind my neck and swayed back to look at me at arm's length. 'There you are, Rupert, fucking can be a most artistic affair when performed by an agile couple. Now, please hold me very tight.'

As I did so, the graceful girl pulled herself towards me and raised the other leg, locking both her legs now around my waist and impaling herself completely upon my delighted prick.

Clinging to me, she nipped and nuzzled my neck as I clasped her to me. She gave a small sigh and wriggled as if to take up a more comfortable position. I clung on to her waist as now she swayed back again but this time let go of my shoulders so that her body was arched backwards with her arms hanging loosely and her fingers trailing on the eiderdown.

Then, as I supported my delicious burden, she slowly pulled her body back up to me, and I could feel the muscles of her back ripple under my hands as she repeated the movement. But this time, as she clung to me again, she lifted herself slightly, taking her weight now on her arms and pressing down but not too heavily upon my shoulders. With her legs still locked around my waist, this enabled her to smooth her cunney in an almost teasing way along my cock. I felt the butterfly touch of her erect little clitty as it rubbed its way exquisitely on my shaft which was made even more slippery by her free-flowing juices.

Diana then began to rotate her hips and we began the inevitable journey towards our climax. I felt her cunt grip my cock even harder as we entered the final stages. She shivered and trembled as she first reached the desired haven and seconds later I too started to spend, spurting my hot jet of love juice inside her and Diana gurgled with joy as the frothy white cream filled her cunney and she shuddered with ecstacy as she milked my twitching tool of every last drop of sticky essence.

We collapsed in a heap on top of Cecily and Frank and we stayed there in a tired but contented tangle of naked limbs. But the girls were not yet sated! Frank and I dug deep into our reserves of strength and produced two fine fresh stiffstanders and we developed an excellent fucking chain with Cecily on her knees, leaning forward to gobble my cock whilst Frank pushed his prick into her cunt from behind whilst he frigged Diana's pussey as the blonde temptress exchanged the most passionate of French kisses with me and I fondled her erect raspberry nipples that were as hard as miniature pricks as I rubbed them between my fingers. To conclude this afternoon of lechery, the two girls lay down again and played with each other's pussies, each fingering the other as Frank and I knelt down to have our cocks sucked, mine by Cecily and Frank by Diana.

So ended Frank's first fuck and for both of us, a valuable lesson in *recherché* fucking. We learned much from this lusty joust, not least perhaps, the necessity to experiment until one finds one's way to best please both oneself and one's partner. This is a most important maxim which I gladly pass on to budding cocksmen both young and not-so-young who may be reading my carnal confessions.

CHAPTER THREE

A Night To Remember

ALL GOOD THINGS COME TO AN END, AS my dear mama was wont to say, and to the chagrin of Frank and myself we only managed one further hectic bout of fucking with Cecily and Diana before the girls were whisked away unexpectedly only three days later by Cecily's parents, Sir Jack and Lady Cardew, to spend the rest of the summer at the sumptuous villa of Lord Zwaig, in the heart of the Dordogne region of southern France. We cursed our luck as we were looking forward to a summer holiday like no other, spending our days exploring the multifarious joys of love-making. However, this was still to be a vintage vacation for my sturdy young cock, for the very same morning that we heard the gloomy news about the impending loss of Cecily and Diana, the weather changed as it so often does in this country and the rain fairly howled down, leaving us no alternative but to spend the entire day indoors. Frank leafed through a copy of *Country Life* whilst I idly explored the books in a cabinet usually kept locked but which, on this afternoon, was unaccountably open.

I picked out a thick volume covered for some reason not with a cloth or leather binding but by a plain wrapping of brown paper. My curiosity was aroused and when I opened the book to my great surprise I discovered that I had chanced upon my father's bound copy of *The Oyster*, an anthology of stories from the most salacious of illicit magazines. I had never actually seen the publication myself but Hammond, the captain of cricket at St Lionel's, once obtained a copy from a sporting acquaintance of his father. Alas, it never reached beyond the exalted studies of the sixth form landing before it was confiscated by our housemaster, Mr Prout, after Hammond had carelessly left it folded inside his Latin text-book. Even more surprising to me was the fact that the book began with a special introduction 'on the delights of good fucking' penned by a frequent visitor to our house, one of my father's oldest and closest friends, that famed traveller of the Indian sub-continent, Professor Grahame Johnstone of Edinburgh University.

[*Not too surprising actually when one considers that Professor Johnstone wrote an erotic novella for* The Oyster *in 1891, a piece very different from his well-known books on various aspects of life in late Victorian India – Editor.*]

'Frank, you must come and look at what I've found here,' I called out excitedly to my friend. 'I can hardly believe it but my pater has been keeping a copy of something really fruity in this bookcase.'

'You don't say,' he said as he ambled over to see for himself. 'Gosh! What kind of book is this?

I've never seen anything like this in my life!' he exclaimed as he riffled through the pages and stopped at a fully coloured illustrated photographic plate. We pored over the picture which had, as its background setting, the inside of a cobbler's shop. In the foreground, in full view of a shocked-looking clerical gentleman peering through the window, an attractive girl was shown on her knees, her breasts bared, pleasuring a happy young fellow whose trousers and drawers were round his ankles and whose veiny cockshaft was being lustily sucked by the comely red-haired miss. The caption under the lascivious photograph was: *'She was only a cobbler's daughter but she gave the boys her awl'*, a jocular play on words made even more amusing by its very rude complementary illustration.

There were several other such photographic plates, all artistically hand-coloured by Michael Harper [*a Scottish-born painter and a highly respected member of the Royal Academy whose services were in great demand during the late Victorian and early Edwardian years and who deemed it prudent to emigrate to the United States in 1906 after his supposed involvement with the Duchess of Cornwall and King Edward VII in an orgy at the home of Elizabeth Thomson, a popular music hall artiste of the Edwardian era – Editor*]. We sat engrossed by this truly superb collection of coloured plates which showed girls and boys in the nude, both singly and together, enjoying themselves in a variety of love-making positions. Even more surprising was the fact that we were certain that one of the models was Mr Newman, the former games master at St Lionel's, who left the school only the year before to take up a similar post at Eton College. If it were another gentleman, I would have been amazed for the likeness to Mr Newman was to the tee, even down to the small appendectomy scar on his stomach.

Frank's cock had now hardened in his trousers and he pulled out his bursting prick to relieve himself by a quick wank. 'Well, well,' I commented, laying my hand around his hot, throbbing shaft. 'What a size yours swells up to these days. It seems to have grown even bigger since your first fuck with Cecily the other day.'

'I do believe you're right, Rupert. I think it's probably about another half inch longer and probably a bit thicker too.'

We then jumped out of our skins as a merry female voice suddenly broke into this lewd conversation. 'So it's Cecily Cardew who you've been having fun and games with, along with Diana Wigmore! I wondered if you'd found a partner for your friend, Master Rupert, or whether Miss Diana would be asked to share her favours!' We looked up to see who was so knowledgeable about our secret – thank goodness it was only Sally, the prettiest of our parlour-maids, whose shapely curves had been in my thoughts during many a tossing-off since she joined our household the previous November.

Sally was a real smasher and I had thought that a great many of our male visitors thought so too – from the vicar, Reverend Lavery, and old Doctor Attenborough, our local medical practitioner, to my Uncle Algernon (Lord Trippett) who always seemed to find some trifling excuse or other which would involve Sally taking something up or bringing something down from his bedroom and always, come to think of it, when my Uncle was in there by himself! One could hardly blame Uncle Algy, for Sally was more than a cut above the ordinary. Her fair-skinned features were well set off by a hint of pretty freckling around her nose. Her light blue eyes sparkled gaily and her tresses of blonde hair were pinned up underneath her black maid's cap. She was perhaps taller than the average and her firm curvaceous figure promised delights galore, especially as she always wore her white blouse with the top buttons open, giving a delicious view of the swell of her proud white breasts.

I was aghast though that Sally appeared to know far more than she should about what Frank and I had been up to over the previous few days. But what could I say? Frank too was similarly tongue-tied, and I must say that he did look rather funny, standing there with his hand round his prick which still stood high and mighty despite the interruption. It was left to Sally to break the ice. Walking towards us and casting an admiring eye on Frank's tremendous tadger, she said: 'So, Master Frank, you think that your cock has grown since you fucked Miss Cecily? Well, you do have a big one for your age, that's for sure – now how would you like me to finish you off?'

Frank found his voice at last. 'I should say so!' he exclaimed as Sally ran her fingers along his visibly palpitating prick. 'Fair shares for all!' I cried, unbuttoning my flies and bringing out my own substantial shaft for her inspection. 'M'm, that's a nice-looking tool as well, Master Rupert, even though it's not quite the size of your friend's. But then, size isn't so important. It's how you put to use what the Lord has blessed you with, as the vicar is always telling me. After all, your father's pal Algy Moncrieffe hasn't got a very big cock at all, but he's probably the best fuck I've ever entertained between my legs, and that's the honest truth.'

With these wise words Sally grasped our two throbbing tools. Poor Frank was already so excited that he spent almost immediately. Sally was only nineteen but this did not prevent her saying regretfully: 'Ah, what a pity, but you young boys can't last out like older men.' However, I did manage to hold on a little longer than Frank before my prick also jetted out a prodigious stream of spunk all over one of Mama's favourite Chinese rugs.

'Damn, how on earth are we going to clean up the carpet?' I wailed but Sally was not flustered by the problem. 'Don't worry, boys, I'll fetch a bottle of Dr Stanton Harcourt's cough medicine and rub in a few drops. Mr Goldhill showed me how to take out sperm and cunney juice stains out of my sheets after he fucked me the day after I joined the staff. You know all butlers have their way with the girls, given half a chance, and I didn't mind obliging – especially as I can always wangle an extra day off here and there from him if I promise that I'll suck his prick some time afterwards!'

So our starched old retainer was another in our household not above enjoying a good fuck, I mused as Sally continued: 'Yes, the mixture's quite marvellous at removing all traces of love-making. It's quite a good weed-killer too, which is worth remembering! Now, take off your trousers so you'll be ready for when I return.'

We not only took off our trousers but also our shoes, socks, shirts and vests so we were both stark naked when Sally returned with the bottle of Dr Stanton Harcourt's magic liquid. 'Oooh, how nice,' she said as she carefully locked the door behind her. 'I'll be with you both just as soon as I've attended to this carpet.'

When she had completed her chore she unbuttoned her blouse completely and shrugged off the garment. She was wearing nothing underneath and we gasped at the sight of the curvy *rondeurs* of her uncovered breasts. How firm and proudly they jutted out and how stalky were her rose-red nipples that she tweaked up against her palms as she lifted the nude beauties as if offering them up to us for closer inspection. What lovely nipples they were, well separated, each looking a little away from each other and tapering in well-proportioned curves until they came to two crimson points set in the pink circles of Sally's aureoles. These taut titties acted as magnets to my hands as I fondled these succulent spheres, rubbing her rubbery red nipples until they were as hard as my stiff cock which was pressing up against her flat tummy.

'Quick, I want you to fuck me before you spend,' she said urgently. She stripped off the rest of her clothes and turned round, bending over so that her glorious bum cheeks were only inches away from my straining knob. She stood with her legs apart and my hands trembled as I parted the chubby soft cheeks, as white as alabaster. I paused for a moment to savour the sight of her pouting cunney lips as they stretched open to reveal the flushed inner flesh of her cunt.

I leaned over her and Sally whimpered as she felt the smooth crown of my cock wedge itself between her buttocks. Before fucking from behind with Cecily and Diana I would have certainly been too shy to attempt a fuck in this fashion but *experientia docet* and she turned her head round to look at me with her limpid blue eyes and murmured: 'Go on, Rupert, fuck me in whatever way takes your fancy!' What a wonderfully open invitation but, as afore-mentioned, I did not attempt to cork her winking little bum-hole. I propelled my prick, which was now as hard as rock, as far forward as I could manage and Sally wiggled to enable my shaft to enter the supple, glistening crack of her cunt. Fiercely, I pushed onwards, burying my cock to the very hilt so that my balls banged against her backside as I pulled back a little before plunging in deep inside her welcoming cunney.

I began to fuck the delicious girl with a quickening pace, my ballsack now slapping against her arse as she cried out with delight, her whole body rocking in rhythm with my cock as it slithered in and out of her juicy pussey which squeezed open and shut like a slippery fist as we thrilled each other with our bodies. I held her round the waist with one hand and leaned round to rub the nipple of one of her magnificent breasts with the other, which excited her greatly. I felt Sally explode into a series of peaks of pleasure as I continued relentlessly to pump in and out of her pussey. Her cunt was incredibly tight and wet and her love-channel clung to my cock as I rode her to the very limit. Again and again I drove home until I felt the familiar surge building up in my balls. At the same time Sally screamed and shuddered to a superb climax as I gushed a torrent of hot spunk into her crack. What a blissful fuck this was and I withdrew my still semi-stiff shaft, which was gleaming with its coating of Sally's pussey juice, and the cheeky girl turned round and chuckled: 'Ten out of ten, Master Rupert, I told you that the size of a prick is relatively unimportant.'

I stroked my penis proudly and Sally took hold of it with both hands and rubbed it between her palms until it regained its full length and strength and rose as hard as iron against my belly. 'Can you carry on for another fuck?' she asked anxiously. When I nodded my assent she gave my sturdy staff a frisk final frigging before laying herself down on a nearby couch. She then told me to come over and lie on top of her and to straddle her body with my legs. I did as I was told and Sally took hold of my pulsating cock, pulling me forwards and I assumed that she was going to suck my throbbing tool. But no, she placed the sticky shaft in the cleft between her breasts and squeezed them around my pole. 'Go on, Master Rupert, fuck my big titties!' she whispered and I began a further lesson in the delights of *l'art de faire l'amour*. I was not over-sure as how best to continue but instead let nature take its course. I rocked my hips to pump my rigid rod up and down the snug cleft of Sally's breasts. It was extraordinarily sensuous, especially when she leaned her face forward and took the crown of my cock and began licking and lapping it as it moved to and fro between her breasts.

'I'm coming! I'm coming!' she wailed, one hand

now dipping between her legs to finger her pussey and the other teasing my balls and arse. 'Oh yes, yes, yes, you're making me come by fucking my titties!'

She threw back her head as she continued moaning and her white teeth gleamed as her lips parted and her eyes closed in ecstasy as she spent profusely. Her blood was still up, though, and the last thing she wanted to do now was to stop this grand sport. But would my now tiring cock be able to continue with this now frenzied fucking? As I now know, there is no strong performance without a touch of fanaticism in the performer. I held on as I found new strength to slide my pole backwards and forwards. She clamped her lips around my knob and sucked hard, sending little electric currents along the shaft. Then she released my knob from her mouth and pushed my shoulders upwards and told me to be still.

Who was I to disobey such a sweetly spoken command? So I lay back and let Sally clamber over me. First she made herself comfortable, sitting astride me and trailing those magnificent breasts up and down my torso as she leaned forward so that her tawny nipples flicked exquisitely across my skin. Then she lifted her hips and crouched over my truncheon which stood high in the air with her cunney directly above my knob. She took hold of my staff and encouragingly rubbed the pulsating pole before cleverly positioning my uncapped helmet so that it pressed directly against her clitty. Rotating her body, she edged forward slightly to allow my rigid rod to enter her. Ever so slowly she lifted and lowered her sopping pussey and each time she sank downwards my cock went deeper and higher inside her until our bodies simply melted away in sheer delight as she lay sated upon me, my prick so fully ensheathed inside her cunt that our pubic hairs were enmeshed together.

I heard Frank draw in his breath sharply and turned my head to see my friend sitting on the edge of his chair, his big prick visibly swelling as he frigged it up to its fullest stiffness. 'Go on Rupert, fuck her juicy cunt,' he muttered. 'And when you've finished perhaps I can have a go!'

Our senses were now at fever pitch. My upward strokes excited her into taking up a fresh, fierce little fucking rhythm as she thrust down to meet my movements to cram every inch of hard cock inside her cunney. Now we both felt the first unmistakable tremors of an approaching spend. Shudder after shudder ran through Sally's quivering body as she half sat back again so that I could best cup her plump breasts in my hands. She gave a choking cry and began to ride up and down on me with a renewed vigour, forcing herself down even harder on my cock. It even crossed my mind that her cries might attract attention from outside the library!

Then I felt that magical first stirrings as my spunk began to force its way up my distended shaft. Sally sensed this and immediately she ceased all movement, her cunt now halfway down my cock as she reached down to kiss me. Twice more she arrested our spends until she was fully ready for her own orgasm. She moved up and down with shorter, faster thrusts and I responded with similar upward jerks. Her mouth was open and she was gaping and moaning as we reached the very brink of ecstacy. Suddenly her cunney muscles tightened about me in a long, rippling seizure that ran from the base to the very root of my cock. Three times more this clutching spasm travelled the entire length of my shaft and then just as Sally screamed out: 'Yes, Yes, Yes! I've come, I've come! Now shoot your spunk, young Rupert!' in a near-delirium, grinding her pussey against me as the frothy jism forced its way out of my knob, hot and seething into every nook and cranny of her cunt.

As we slowly subsided, panting and near collapse, we lay entwined in an intimate jumble of bare flesh. Though I could hear a series of rapid knocks on the door (thank goodness Sally had locked it!), a warm wave of fatigue washed over me and I just could not bring myself to even answer the insistent unknown caller.

Fortunately Frank was still *compos mentis* and I could not help smiling as he heaved himself out of his chair and padded naked across to the door, stiff frigging his stiff cock which was raised as high as a flagpole against his tummy. 'Who's there?' he asked. 'It's Goldhill, sir,' came the voice of our old butler. 'I'm sorry to disturb you but I have a message to give to Master Rupert from his father.'

Even at the early age of fifteen and a half, Frank was one of the most quick-witted chaps I have ever known. With only a brief pause, itself covered by a clearing of his throat, he replied: 'Ah, well, Goldhill, I'm afraid Rupert's just fallen asleep and I don't really want to disturb him which is why I locked the door. You see, he was complaining about having a slight headache and hopefully he'll sleep it off.'

87

'I distinctly thought I heard noises coming from the library.'

'So you did,' said Frank. 'Rupert was talking in his sleep and I think he must have been having a nightmare! Is the matter of great urgency or can you come back in ten minutes?'

So thanks to Frank's fast-thinking we had time to dress ourselves and for Sally to sneak out of the library, undetected by Goldhill or any of the other servants. When Goldhill made his second appearance ten minutes later as requested, I made a great show of yawning and stretching out my arms. 'Frank has told me that you have a message from Papa,' I said. 'I hope that it wasn't too urgent as I had a beastly pri–, I mean, headache and needed forty winks. But I'm all right now, thank goodness.' I added though I noticed that this had not prevented the butler from shooting me a suspicious look.

'Yes, Master Frank told me about it. I am glad you have recovered so quickly. The Colonel and Mrs Mountjoy are attending the annual general meeting of the Yorkshire Society For The Promotion Of Science in Harrogate and they have asked me to tell you that they are expecting a visitor to arrive here early this afternoon. On their behalf, they ask you to extend every hospitality to this gentleman as your parents do not expect to return until about half past three as they are taking luncheon today with Lord and Lady Beasant in Bilton. Our new guest, who will be staying here for a few days, is a Mr Frederick Nolan, an American gentleman from California. You may be interested to know, Master Rupert, that Mr Nolan will be bringing with him one of these new-fangled cinematographs. If you know what I mean, sir, these are the machines that take moving pictures.'

'Moving pictures,' echoed Frank. 'Well, what a coincidence! I was reading about them in the *Manchester Guardian* only this morning. Is this Mr Nolan going to give us an exhibition of his work?'

'Yes, sir,' intoned Goldhill. 'Indeed it was Mr Nolan who wrote the article you read in the newspaper. He is in Yorkshire to make a film on the Dales which he intends to show to audiences in America.'

'Wow, perhaps we can be in it?' said Frank excitedly. 'Wouldn't that be great?'

'I doubt it as the sight of your face would crack the camera lens!' I replied with a laugh.

'Ha, ha, ha – well, you can laugh but I'm jolly well going to ask him if I can help in any way,' responded my chum. 'Goldhill, is there anything we must prepare for Mr Nolan's arrival?'

'No, sir,' said the butler. 'I will be sure to let you both know when Mr Nolan arrives.'

Goldhill did not have to carry out this task, for we were so keen to meet Mr Nolan that we bolted through luncheon and when the doorbell rang just after two o'clock Frank and I raced to the front door to welcome our American guest in style.

I opened the door to a handsome gentleman in the prime of life, perhaps a mite shorter in height than the average, dressed in a snappy summer suit and carrying a silver topped walking stick. 'Good afternoon, sir. You must be Mr Nolan, the cinematographer. Welcome to Albion Towers.'

'That's right, young man, Fred Nolan at your service, all the way from the USA. And who may you be?'

'I'm Rupert Mountjoy, sir, the Colonel's son. And this is my friend, Frank Folkestone.'

'Glad to meet you, Frank,' said the genial stranger, beckoning to his driver to unload the cart which contained his luggage and two large chests which no doubt contained all his cinematographic equipment.

'I'll have someone bring in all your cases, sir,' I said.

'Well, thank you, my boy, but I'll supervise the operation, if you don't mind. My cameras must be handled very carefully.'

After we had helped Mr Nolan to settle in, he gratefully accepted the offer of some refreshment. Goldhill brought in a large whisky and soda and Mrs Randall provided a platter of cold roast beef sandwiches and a pot of hot black coffee. I apologised for my parents' absence but Mr Nolan waved aside my words: 'No need to apologise, you've done me proud, young man, though I look forward to meeting your parents. Now before they come I'd very much like to take a walk around your estate whilst the rain holds off.'

'Are you planning the scenario for a film?' I asked.

'Yup, that's the idea. My boy, motion pictures are in their infancy and the three-minute film will, I predict, soon be overtaken by full-length plays which will be shown in special movie theatres,' he replied.

We must have looked dubious for Mr Nolan continued: 'I see you doubt me. Well, boys, I'll go further, I will go so far as to predict that motion pictures will in your lifetime be seen in colour and you'll be able to hear the spoken word coming out from the screen! Ah, I see you smile – well, we shall see, we shall see. Just remember that people laughed at Mr Edison's idea for a phonograph [*or gramophone as the British called the early record-players – Editor*].

'But that probably won't happen until the dawn of the new century. Right now, how would you like to come out with me to look for a suitable location for my film?'

'I should say,' said Frank with alacrity, 'especially if we could later watch you make your film.'

'Of course, of course,' said Mr Nolan cordially. 'If you like, you may even appear in it!' The promise of such a treat was more than enough to get us out of doors and we tramped round our garden until Mr Nolan stopped and said: 'This looks like the perfect spot. I want to take a shot of the house before pointing the camera at a tea-party taking place on the lawn. If the weather is good enough and your parents are amenable, we will made a start directly after breakfast.'

My parents arrived home soon afterwards and, like Frank and myself, they thoroughly enjoyed the company of the gregarious American who regaled us with a flood of anecdotes about his fascinating life. Mr and Mrs Harbottle and their daughter Katie had also been invited to dine with us and I could see that Katie, a slim, attractive girl of twenty-one, who was sitting next to Mr Nolan, was especially taken with his recounting of his adventures. It seemed that Mr Nolan's late father was one of the railway magnates back in America and being the sole heir to a very considerable fortune had enabled his son to travel the world at his leisure.

'You must find it very dull here after New York, Rome, Paris and London, Mr Nolan,' sighed my Mama who unlike Papa, enjoyed the bustle of town life, having been brought up in London.

He shook his head. 'Dull? Not a bit of it, ma'am, it's a real pleasure to be able to enjoy the peace and quiet of the country. Why, in New York, or in any great city, I don't think it is possible to secure even six hours of undisturbed sleep. I certainly never achieved this last week in London. I can't blame anyone for the choir of cats that decided to hold a concert on the roof of my hotel but I could have cheerfully strangled the two cabbies who careered down Marylebone High Street shouting imprecations to each other that I cannot repeat here!'

As he paused to take a glass of champagne from Goldhill, I bent under the table to retrieve my napkin which had fallen to the floor. And what a shock I had as I looked across to see that Katie Harbottle, who was sitting opposite Mr Nolan, and who was a most pleasant but quiet and shy girl in company, had taken off her right shoe and was running her stockinged toes up and down Mr Nolan's left leg! Yet the American continued this little tale as if nothing untowards was happening even though Katie's foot, hidden from general view, was now caressing his inner thigh and was rising higher towards his groin with every stroke!

I could hardly remain under the table but, as I straightened up, Mr Nolan continued as if nothing untoward was happening: 'Then one has to cope with the rumbling thunder made by the dustmen's carts, to say nothing of the infernal row made by drunken revellers pouring out of the clubs. Oh, I could think of a hundred other sleep-preventers as well.'

'I can think of a better sleep-preventer than all that – Sally the parlourmaid sucking my cock!' muttered Frank, who was sitting besides me. I dropped my napkin, deliberately this time, and when I bent down to pick it up, I drew a sharp breath to prevent an exclamation of amazement escape from my lips. Katie was still rubbing one foot down Mr Nolan's leg, but now he had brazenly opened the buttons of his flies, and this was allowing Katie to wriggle the toes of her other foot inside his trousers, stroking them against his naked rampant penis which stood up stiffly out of his under-shorts.

With difficulty I suppressed the urge to succumb to hysterics, though I wondered wildly how the two of them would extricate themselves from this compromising situation. Surprisingly enough, it proved far less awkward than I envisaged for when the time came for the ladies to retire, Katie simply slipped her shoes back on and left the room together with the two older ladies. Mr Nolan did not rise fully as the ladies left the table but crouched over his chair, hastily buttoning his trousers as Goldhill came in with a tray of liqueurs.

'Do you belong to any clubs here in England, Mr Nolan?' asked my father, as Goldhill poured out cognac for us all (Frank and I were allowed a small measure as a special treat) and Mr Nolan nodded his head. 'Yes, I belong to the Reform and the Travellers and my club in Washington, D.C., the Beesknees, has connections with the Jim Jam in London.'

'The Jim Jam,' said my father thoughtfully. 'I don't think I've ever heard of that establishment.'

Mr Nolan looked quickly at Frank and myself and hurriedly changed the subject: 'I don't get there very often, Colonel. Tell me now, how do you occupy your time since you left the Indian Army?'

[*It is hardly surprising that Mr Nolan had no wish to elaborate further upon his membership of the Jim Jam Club, a semi-secret gentlemen's* maison closé *situated in Great Windmill Street, Soho. The uninhibited revelries that took place there (King Edward VII was a frequent visitor in his younger days as Prince of Wales) were commented upon with relish in several underground magazines of the era including the notorious* Intimate Memoirs of Dame Jenny Everleigh *recently republished by Sphere Books, London – Editor.*]

'I'm enjoying the life of an English country gentleman,' replied my father. 'Plenty of hunting, shooting and fishing, you know.'

'Are you keen on country pursuits, Mr Nolan?' asked George Harbottle, Katie's father and the local squire who was perhaps the best shot in the entire county, a fact that was best kept from Mr Nolan whose only pursuit this evening was fucking the squire's daughter!

'As an American I'm always at ease in the great outdoors, sir, and have always been extremely fond of the country,' said Frederick Nolan with a smile.

'Well, it's true that he's extremely fond of cunt!' I said softly to Frank.

'Why, what are you talking about?' my friend whispered back. I quietly explained what I had seen going on underneath the table, which made Frank choke with laughter.

'Let us all in on the joke, boys,' said my father genially.

Frank again showed his uncanny ability to manoeuvre his way out of a tight corner by explaining that the cognac had 'gone down the wrong way' and we sat quietly whilst the others finished their liqueurs. 'Shall we join the ladies?' said my father, rising from his seat and as neither guest had taken up my father's previous offer of a cigar, we trooped into the drawing room. Not surprisingly the conversation came round to Mr Nolan's films and Frank and I exchanged a knowing glance when Katie Harbottle said: 'I'd very much like to see your equipment, Mr Nolan.'

'Ah, that creates a slight problem,' said the cunning cinematographer, 'You see, I have set everything up in my room and it would be rather difficult to bring it all downstairs.'

Katie looked disappointed but Mrs Harbottle said: 'I don't see why you could not go up to Mr Nolan's room and see his equipment there.'

'I say, Enid –' spluttered her husband, but she imperiously waved away his protest. 'Really, George, by refusing Katie permission to go with Mr Nolan you are, unwittingly of course, insulting them both! Do you feel that Mr Nolan or your daughter would behave improperly just because they would be alone for fifteen minutes?'

I wondered who was silently cheering Mrs Harbottle's progressive views – my Mama, who had persuaded Mrs Harbottle of the justice of the Suffragette cause (much to the squire's disgust!), or Katie and Frederick Nolan who I knew would like nothing better than to find themselves together in a private place and especially a bedroom!

So the young couple made good their escape and at the same time Frank and I were given leave to go and play ping pong [*table tennis – Editor*] on the new table my father had bought me for my birthday last February. On our way to the games room, I suddenly remembered that the other day I had noticed that the bats were missing so I said: 'Come downstairs, Frank and we'll find Goldhill. He'll know where the blinking bats have been put away.' Everyone on duty must have been in the kitchen as there was no member of staff to greet us at the foot of the stairs. However, we heard a girl giggling and then a short murmur coming from a room in front of us. 'That sounds like Goldhill,' I said so we followed the sounds and pushed open the door of the servants' sitting room. I don't know who was the most embarrassed, Frank and myself or Goldhill and Polly, the scullery maid. For the dark-haired girl was sprawled naked on the large sofa with Goldhill, who was still in uniform (except for his trousers and drawers which were lying over his ankles) slewing his prick in and out of her hairy pussey. At first we stood unseen as the butler's lean bottom cheeks pumped up and down while the couple rocked in time with their amorous exertion. Then Polly let out a little scream as she saw us standing there, gaping at this lewd scene.

'Don't mind us, old fellow,' Frank called out. 'We'd much rather wait until you've finished before attending to us.'

'Yes, attend to Polly first, Goldhill,' I said, rather enjoying the butler's discomforture though I noted that Polly seemed little put out by the interruption. 'Her need is greater than ours.'

Polly giggled. 'Come on then, Mr Goldhill, let's take up where we left off!' And to encourage him she turned over to lie face downwards, reaching across for a soft cushion to insert under her belly so that her hips and chubby rounded bum cheeks were raised high in the air. The butler shuffled between her legs and nudging her knees part, took his sizeable stalk in his hand. 'Are you ready then, Polly?' he asked and after receiving a quick nod of assent, he carefully guided his gleaming weapon into the crack between her bum cheeks, his knob brushing up against her cunney lips before sliding through them into the warm wetness of her welcoming cunt.

I must say that Goldhill was no slouch when it came to the mark. As soon as his prick was safely ensheathed in Polly's pussey the butler began to fuck her at a slowish but regular pace and leaned forward so that his chest lay on Polly's back. He reached round to fiddle with her large tawny titties, holding them in thrall as he continued to slew his cock in and out of her sopping slit. Her backside slapped enticingly against his surprisingly muscular thighs as she slipped into the rhythm of fucking that he had established and he increased the pace, now forcefully pounding away as Polly wriggled in delight.

As you may imagine, friendly reader, the sight of his thick, veined member see-sawing in and out of her willing cunney made Frank and I extremely horney, especially when the rude girl reached behind to grab hold of his swinging ballsack as it slapped against her bum. Sensing that she was waiting for him, Goldhill increased the speed of his fucking once more and he croaked: 'Here it comes, Polly, brace yourself!' as his torso went rigid and his twitching tool expelled its emission of frothy jism into her seething crack. Polly yelped with glee as the glorious sensations of her own impending orgasm swept like magic throughout her body. The butler collapsed on top of the delighted maid who twisted her bum lasciviously to draw out the last drains of sperm from Goldhill's now exhausted cock.

'Now that was a marvellous fuck, let's do it again,' said Polly brightly but our old retainer looked disconcertedly down at his shrunken shaft and shook his head.

'I'm sorry, but I'm not up to it, my girl. Besides, I've got to do some work for Master Rupert,' he said as he pulled up his trousers.

'Oh dear,' wailed the gorgeous girl. 'Is there not a single stiff prick in the entire house?'

This question was immediately answered by Frank who fairly ripped open the buttons of his fly to bring out his huge naked cockshaft. 'Will this do?' he enquired, bringing his giant tool closer for Polly to inspect, making the purple knob leap and bound in his hand.

'Oooh, that looks good enough to eat,' said Polly, sliding down on her knees from the sofa and weighing Frank's meaty staff in the palm of her hand. 'What an enormous penis for a lad as young as you!' she exclaimed. I was now getting a little miffed at hearing all the girls say this as soon as Frank showed his cock to any female either upstairs or downstairs!

'Would you like me to suck it or would this mean you wouldn't be able to fuck me afterwards?' she asked.

'Do put it in your mouth, I'll come twice without

any problems,' he answered eagerly and on hearing such good news she popped his swollen helmet into her mouth. I could see that Polly was a brilliant *fellatrice*. She worked on his knob with her tongue, easing her lips forward to take in a little of his shaft. She encircled the base of his cock with one hand and with the other, she began to work the pink, velvety skin up and down, her head bobbing as she sucked away with undisguised relish, taking as much of his rigid pole as she could manage between her lips. Her warm breath and moist mouth sent Frank into the seventh heaven of delight and the feel of her wet tongue slithering around his tingling tool soon brought my chum to the brink of a spend. His tadger jerked uncontrollably as she now moved her hands from his cock to grasp the firm, muscular cheeks of his bottom, moving him backwards and forwards until with a final juddering throb he spurted a lavish stream of sperm into her welcoming mouth. She swallowed his emission joyfully, smacking her lips as she gulped down his tangy jism.

'Now, Master Frank, is your young cock still up to the mark as you promised it would be?' gasped Polly as she cast herself back on the sofa, her legs wide apart to expose her pouting pussey and the receptive red slash of cunney flesh which made my already swollen prick strain even more unmercifully against the material of my trousers. I must confess that I wondered whether Frank could fulfil his boast after squirting his spunk so powerfully down Polly's throat but my doubts were quickly assuaged as Frank, his cock waggling, clambered upon the girl's rich curves with hardly a pause. A moan from them both signalled that his knob had slipped between her cunney lips without any preliminaries. He withdrew and then pushed in again slowly and I saw how, parting slowly to his push, the velvet lips appeared to draw him in as their mouths met in the most passionate of kisses. The bold minx jerked her bottom to absorb more of his slippery staff and in a trice, with a cry of bliss, he was fully engulfed inside the sweet prison of her cunt, his hairy ballsack dangling against her plump backside.

Frank's slim, smooth body moved in rhythm, faster and faster until the naughty pair were rocking furiously as he now pounded his thick, rock-hard prick into her willing juicy love channel. Polly twisted in veritable throes of ecstacy, panting and grunting with delight as she slipped her hands down Frank's back to grasp his bum cheeks, eagerly lifting her hips to welcome the thrusting shaft that was sliding so deliciously in and out of her sopping cunney.

'Oh yes, what a glorious fuck! What a strong young cock you have! Faster, faster, I want all that lovely jism in your balls, fill me up with it, flood my cunney!' she gasped.

Quite berserk, the lewd couple rolled around on the sofa as Frank's delighted penis slewed joyously in and out of her honeypot. 'There I go!' she squealed, and Frank tensed his frame as with a cry he crashed down one final time upon Polly's quivering body, his cock jetting spasms of spunk streaming inside her slit as she squeezed her thighs together and milked every last drop of jism from his spurting stalk. She showed no signs of releasing him until his penis started to deflate and only then did she allow him to pull it out of her drenched cunney.

I would have liked nothing better at that moment then to have fucked Polly myself especially as I could see that her eyes were looking directly at the bulge between my legs as my stiffened prick twitched uncomfortably in the confines of my trousers. But Goldhill cleared his throat and murmured: 'I suggest that we all leave here as soon as possible, the other servants will be returning at any time.' We could not ignore his warning so Polly and Frank began to dress and I turned to Goldhill to ask him where the table tennis bats might be found. He told me that they were kept with a bag of ping pong balls in a cupboard on the landing just outside the games room.

'Do you still fancy a game, Frank, or are you now too tired?' I laughed.

'No, no, I'll happily play with you,' he said, buttoning up his fly buttons, 'although I'll tell you now that it won't be as much fun as playing with Polly!'

'No, I bet it won't,' I said sourly. 'I would have liked to have judged the difference myself.'

'Now, now, Master Rupert, don't be jealous,' smiled Polly. 'Look, I tell you what, I'll come up to your room at eleven o'clock tonight and we'll all have some fun.'

'*All* have some fun?' I queried.

'Oh, yes,' she said gaily. 'Master Frank must be there or I won't come. He has the most amazing prick –'

'Yes, yes, I know, it's so big for a boy his age.' I

101

said heavily, but I wasn't really too put out at yet a further compliment given to Frank's huge penis. After all, my friend's cock was paving the way for my own prick to find its way between Polly's legs and so far, none of the girls who I had so far fucked – Diana, Cecily nor Sally – had made the slightest disparaging remark about the prowess of my cock and had indeed praised highly its abilities whilst performing *l'art de faire l'amour*.

This incident first showed me how important it is to know that there will always be a fellow with more notches on his cockshaft than yours; just as there will always be bigger pricks and heavier ballsacks than yours to be seen in the sports club's changing rooms. But at the same time, there will always be those with tinier tadgers and it must be stressed that there are even some young men blessed with members the size of cucumbers who would gladly give their all to have taken part in the number of sexual experiences that you have enjoyed. Of course, I did not fully appreciate this maxim fully at this early stage in my sexual education but I do so now *in toto* and urge its acceptance to all gallant gentlemen.

In fact, it turned out that I had only a couple of hours to wait until my carnal appetite was totally sated by the exquisite Polly Aysgarth who, I will tell you now, dear reader, left our service shortly afterwards to take up a position in Lord Borehamwood's establishment down in London. Roger, his Lordship's youngest son, became infatuated with the sensuous parlourmaid and proposed marriage. Rather than attract the publicity that would be certain to occur if Polly

102

went ahead with a breach-of-contract suit, his Lordship settled the affair by giving Polly four thousand pounds and sending the Honourable Roger off to Australia. Happily, all worked out for the best as Polly settled down in an admittedly unconventional form of marriage with the Russian *roué* Count Sasha Motkalevich and Roger is now one of the most prosperous sheep farmers in New South Wales.

Back however, to my story – on our way upstairs Frank and I heard the sounds of giggling coming from Mr Nolan's quarters and it sounded as though Katie Harbottle was enjoying her private view of Fred Nolan's equipment. However, being gentlemen, we did not eavesdrop and marched on through to the games room. False modesty is just as foolish as overweaning pride, so I will not disguise the fact that I easily vanquished Frank at table tennis, even though he was the best all-round sportsman in my form. We played snooker for a while but neither of us were good enough to make a game of it so we decided to wander back to the drawing room. We met Fred Nolan and Katie just coming out of his room and he looked somewhat flushed of face whilst she was busying herself doing up the buttons of her dress.

'Did you find Mr Nolan's equipment of interest, Miss Harbottle?' I enquired as we approached them.

Without batting an eyelid, she replied sweetly: 'Oh yes indeed, I was quite overwhelmed by the sight of his accoutrements.'

'I'll bet she was, the naughty girl,' I murmured to Frank as we passed by them. The Harbottles left shortly afterwards and Frank and I retired in good time for my chum to be able to dash unseen into my room after changing into his pyjamas.

'I've only cleaned my teeth as I thought I could take a shower after we've fucked Polly,' he said, taking off his dressing gown. I was already eagerly anticipating Polly's arrival and was sitting naked on the bed. Frank decided to slip off his pyjamas, too, as the night was very warm. When we had waited for Diana and Cecily I had been totally confident that they would appear but for some reason I had a nagging doubt as to whether our lusty parlourmaid would keep her word. But I need not have worried because on the stroke of eleven there was an urgent tap on the door. I leaped down and opened the door a fraction – yes, it was Polly, also clothed simply in a dressing gown and looking anxiously up and down the hallway to make sure that she had not been seen.

'Quick, come inside!' I whispered and after she had slipped in I closed the door behind her.

She sat on the bed and looked at Frank and myself. 'Well, boys, here I am and I hope that you two are good and ready for a good night's fucking because I feel very, very randy!' she said, letting the dressing gown fall from her shoulders to slide gracefully down her body. What a wonderful creation the human form is, I marvelled as, very deliberately, Polly traced her hands over her plump yet firm breasts before letting her fingers find their way around her belly and towards her dark, glossy pussey bush. Polly smiled knowingly as she rubbed her thumb against her pouting lips and flashed a saucy smile at us. 'Well, boys, do you approve of the goods on display or do you wish to return them to the manufacturer?' This was a somewhat rhetorical question for already both our cocks were standing smartly to attention and Polly inspected them critically. She was a happy, chatty kind of girl and she prattled away cheerfully as she took our two stiff pricks in her hands and rubbed them up to bursting point.

'M'm, these are two very good-looking cocks. I must admit, and I'm going to enjoy fucking and sucking them. But which one should I start with? Frank, yours is the biggest but size isn't everything. After all, Mr Goldhill hasn't got a very big one either but he always manages to bring me off time after time which is more than your Uncle Martin did, Master Rupert, last time he was at Albion Towers. As Captain Luton down in the village – you know him, I believe, the old sailor who keeps the Fox and Feather Inn – is fond of saying, "It isn't the size of the ship that matters, it's the motion of the ocean!" So I think we'll start off with your prick, Master Rupert, and see what it tastes like. But don't fret, Master Frank, I won't leave you out of it!'

And without further ado she swooped down, clamping her luscious lips around the red mushroomed crown of my cock whilst she grasped Frank's massive shaft at its base and started to wank the rigid rod as she sucked lustily away at my uncapped helmet, washing her tongue over the sensitive knob until I thought I would faint away with the pleasure of it all. I groaned and pressed her curly-haired head downwards until her lips enclosed almost all my throbbing shaft and she dipped her head up and down with a regular motion that sent waves of pure ecstasy rolling out from my groin.

I saw Frank's hand snake out towards Polly's pussey as she continued to rub his stiffstander. She wriggled across so that his fingers could play in her shiny muff. 'Well done, that's the way!' she gasped as he nudged his forefinger against her cunney lips and entered her moist cunt. He pushed first one and then two fingers deeper inside her love-box as she raised her hips up, panting breathlessly as he began to establish a rhythm. Her head continued to bob up and down over my twitching tool until I felt a great shudder of pleasure run through me and I shot a stream of hot spunk down her throat. Polly milked my prick expertly, sucking out every drop of frothy white essence out of my cock whilst Frank continued to play with her juicy cunney as she gripped his hands between her thighs and squeezed it hard against her dripping crack.

Polly smacked her lips and said: 'Master Rupert, your jism is less salty than your friend's, so even if his prick is bigger, your spunk tastes sweeter. There, does that make you feel better?'

Then without waiting for a reply, she turned her attention to Frank for she must have realised from the throbbing of his tool that he would soon shoot off if she carried on masturbating his manly pole. So she lay back on the bed and parted her thighs as Frank clambered on top of her to press his purple knob against her cunney lips. I took hold of his giant shaft and guided it home, sliding the head of the veiny rammer. He sank into her cunt with a grateful sigh of relief.

Once his cock was totally enclosed in her channel Polly closed her thighs, making Frank open his legs and lie astride her with his penis well and truly trapped inside her pussey. 'I love doing this,' Polly panted lewdly. 'Now you just fuck away, young Frank, and let me feel your big prick rub against the sides of my cunt!' However, Frank could scarcely move his cock as the muscles of her cunney were gripping his shaft so tightly but he was happy enough as Polly began to grind her hips round, massaging his prick as it throbbed away inside her cunt which by now was dribbling its love juices down her thighs. I was now desperate to join the fun and games but my cock was still hanging limp. Then suddenly I had a bright idea and slid my hand under Polly's backside and inserted my forefinger in her bum-hole. My precipitate action surprised but in no way upset Polly, who wiggled delightedly upon my finger and squealed: 'You naughty boy, Master Rupert, who's been teaching you about bum-fiddling then!' For some reason this set off Frank and so Polly shifted her thighs and eased the pressure around his raging prick. My chum began to drive wildly now, in and out, in and out like a steamhammer, fucking at such intense speed that I knew he would soon send his gushings of foaming sperm flying out into Polly's sopping slit.

Meanwhile, Polly was being brought off all the time, building herself up to a tremendous orgasm as the fierce momentum of Frank's fucking made her pussey disgorge a veritable rivulet of love juice. She brought her legs up against the small of his back as I continued to jab my finger in and out of her arse-hole. Frank now bore down on her yet again, his body now gleaming with perspiration, fucking that juicy pussey faster and faster, the rippling movement of his cock sliding at breakneck speed against the glistening skin of her cunney. Then with a groan he spurted his seed, drenching her cunt with his jism as Polly quickly closed her thighs together again as he released his entire copious emission, not releasing him until his tool lay still, shrinking back to its natural flaccidness inside her.

Polly wriggled up and rolled the unresisting body of Frank on to the side. 'Now, now, boys, we've only just started! Master Rupert, your cock looks just about ready for another game!' She took hold of my burgeoning prick which was by now stirring anew and it swelled up to its full proud proportions in her fist. She then lay back and drew her legs apart to expose the mark as I took my place on top of her. I glued my lips to hers and clutched her swelling breasts in my hands as she kept firm hold on my cock, ready to place it in position – but she had no need to do so, for the combination of her own and Frank's juices had prepared the oven for the dish, so to speak, and had made her pussey so slippery that my cock immediately slid right in deep inside her cunney without any preliminaries whatsoever. As soon as I felt my cock ensconced in her wet, throbbing sheath I began to heave and shove to our mutual enjoyment. Through the intensity of the sucking off she had previously given me, I was able to prolong the ride, bringing the trembling girl off twice before I added my own sticky liquid tribute to the pungent blobs of love juice that had formed all around her pussey lips and in her furry tuft of cunney hair. I slicked my still stiff shaft in and out of her willing cunt until Polly said: 'Hold hard, Master Rupert, it looks like Frank's cock is rising up again. I think we can now all three play together now, won't that be fun?'

'I should say so,' said Frank, brandishing his erection in his hands and offering up the tip of his prick for Polly to suck. She slurped her lips over his bare red knob, liberally coating it with spittle before saying: 'I want you to fuck my bottom with that big cock of yours, Master Frank.'

She leaned over so that both Polly and I were lying on our sides, for I was still threading her juicy pussey whilst the above conversation was taking place, but this new position allowed her to thrust her chubby buttocks out as I bucked my way into her cunt. Frank then grasped her bum cheeks and parted the rounded globes so that the tiny wrinkled brown orifice between them was fully exposed. He manoeuvered the glowing knob of his proud cock between the adorable cheeks of her ripe derrière and eased it blissfully within the puckered rim of her rear dimple.

'Aaah! Oooh! Aaaah! It's going in! You've filled me up, you randy little fucker!' she cried as Frank urged his cock majestically upwards and inwards into her willing bottom. Polly twisted in delicious agonies as her backside yielded to this attack, grinding her cheeks against Frank's boyish flat belly. At one stage we both pushed our cocks in together and I felt my own staff rubbing against Frank's with only the thin divisional membrane of Polly's cunney and bum-hole running between us. I came first, pumping jet after jet of frothy white spunk while Polly and Frank continued to writhe in new paroxyms of pleasure as Frank corked her bottom, stirring her blood so hotly that she spent copiously as she panted out: 'Come on, Frank, shoot your sperm up my bum. Ooh, that's right, work your shaft in and out whilst you rub my titties!' Frank rammed away in earnest whilst her bottom bounced upon his belly and his sturdy cock eased back and forth between her tightened cheeks until he deluged her little bum-hole with his spoutings, letting Polly climb once more to the very summit of the mountain of love in a final tremulous orgasm.

We continued to revel in such voluptuous delights until our pricks were simply incapable of further use to the insatiable wench, even when she crammed both of our stalks into her mouth and attempted to suck them up again to fresh erections. Ye Gods! What a fizzling fucker was young Polly Aysgarth, a girl who taught me that to fully enjoy the pleasures of love-making, it is necessary to cast aside all mental restraints, for man was made for woman and woman was made for man and as for the parsons and other do-gooders who can only cavil at mutual enjoyment of 'The Sins Of The Flesh', well, the more fool, they!

Polly left us shortly after two o'clock in the morning to sleep away the rest of the night in her own room. I was concerned that she would be reprimanded for not working well the next day, for she would have to be up at six o'clock sharp if not before, and less than four hours' sleep is insufficient for a hard-working servant. But Polly informed us that she had already arranged with Mr Goldhill that if he would not disturb her until noon, she would suck his cock as soon as she had woken up, which sounded a most equitable arrangement to my way of thinking.

Frank was too tired even to put on his pyjamas, let alone to retire to his own room, so we snuggled up together, quite nude, under the eiderdown. I was the first to wake, and though my balls had been emptied more times than I could remember the night before, miraculously they were full again and my cock was standing up majestically to attention. I looked down and saw that Frank's truncheon was in the same fine condition. He was still half-asleep when I took his hand and brought it down to my stiffstander, and he moved his fingers in compliance once I had moved them up and down my tingling staff. I then grasped hold of my pal's tremendous tadger and pumped away with my fist. Simultaneously we spent together, our cocks spurting their gummy essence over the sparse covering of hair around the bases of our shafts and onto our bellies.

'Damn, we've made the sheet sticky,' said Frank. I peered down and said: 'I wouldn't worry, old boy, look how stained the sheet is from last night cavortings!' But before Frank could reply, there was a brisk knock-knock at the door and in came Sally with my early morning cup of tea.

Frank dived beneath the bed-clothes as she put the tray down and went over to the windows to pull open the curtains. 'Good morning, Master Rupert,' she said cheerily. 'Wake up now, it's gone eight o'clock and it's time to get up.' She moved across to the bed and of course immediately saw through Frank's inadequate camouflage. 'Who's that in bed with you, then?' she asked brightly. 'Let's have a look.' And before I could prevent it, she threw back the eiderdown to discover that it was Frank cowering besides me and that we were both naked.

'Dear me, I would have thought you two were old enough and experienced enough to prefer real fucking to playing with each other,' she said reproachfully.

'We are too,' muttered Frank, 'but I was too sleepy from all the fucking last night to go back to my room.'

'Well, it's just as well I came in here first,' commented Sally, 'for if I had gone into your room and found that the bed had not been slept in, I might have raised the alarm and then goodness knows what might have happened.'

'Thank goodness you didn't, Sally, we're very grateful.' I said, covering Frank and myself up with the eiderdown.

'You don't have to be shy! she said. 'I've seen what you've got to offer before, remember? I'm a bit miffed, though, that you didn't tell me that there was some fucking going on because I would have loved to have joined in. Who was with you? It couldn't have been Katie Harbottle because I saw her leave with her parents and anyhow she fancies that spry Yankee gentleman Mr Nolan.'

You can't keep anything secret from the servants, I thought, but when Sally asked me again which girls had been sharing our bed I shook my head. 'You wouldn't like it if it had been you and someone else had asked the next day,' I said reprovingly.

'You're quite right, Master Rupert. It's a right

good maxim for both boys and girls never to tell your friends who you're fucking, unless they pass on the clap in which case you must tell everybody who'll listen to you.' She may have only been a humble servant-girl but her pithy, blunt words should always be remembered by those engaged in any kind of fucking.

Sally looked again and saw that some of the spunk stains on the sheet were fresh. 'Have you two just been tossing each other off? What a pity, I'm sure you would have enjoyed it even more if you'd have let me do it for you.'

'I'm sure we would have done, Sally,' agreed Frank with a touch of sarcasm in his voice as he tried unsuccessfully to rub his tool up to its former stiffness for her approval. 'But then we didn't know you would be bringing us early morning tea let alone providing any hand relief.'

'Oh yes, I wank any gentlemen guests at Albion Towers who request my services,' said Sally as she sat down on the bed. 'I would have seen to that American Mr Nolan but he was taking a bath when I knocked on his door and he didn't ask me to do anything for him except to shut the door behind me when I left his room.'

I looked at her in disbelief. 'What about Mama's cousins, the Reverend Horace Dumpole, who stayed with us for a week earlier this year? You're surely not telling –'

She laughed heartily at my naivety. 'The Reverend Horace? Surely you must be joking, Master Rupert. Why, he was one of the gamest boys I've ever seen. After he found out what I would do for him, every morning regular as clockwork he'd be lying naked on his bed waiting

113

for me, fondling his shaft as if he could hardly wait. Mind, he was shy at first,' she added thoughtfully. 'What happened was that on the second day of his visit I took him his tea and when I leaned over to put down the tray, I made sure he got a good look at my breasts. I'd kept the top buttons undone, you see, and my chemise was cut so low that he could easily hardly fail to see my titties when I bent over him. I could see how excited he was because his hands were shaking so much when I gave him his tea that he spilled most of it into the saucer! Anyhow, I took the cup away and told him to take off his nightshirt as he'd spilled tea all over it and it would be best if I put it in the wash straightaway.

'He protested at first but after a little persuasion off came the nightshirt. But as he handed it to me you will never guess what I noticed lying on the bed – it was a copy of *The Intimate Memoirs Of Jenny Everleigh*! "My, my," I joked. "I would have thought that this was rather a rude book for a Man of the Cloth." He blushed a deep shade of puce and said: "Ah, yes, er, yes, well, the truth of the matter is that I borrowed this book to illustrate to my flock what kind of unsuitable material there is available at certain bookshops and how careful good people must be not to buy such publications in error when for example they might wish to purchase *The Recollections of Reverend James Everleigh*, the former Bishop of Swaziland, which is a very different volume indeed, I can assure you."

' "I'm sure it is, your Reverence," I giggled, "and I'm sure it is a very worthy book as well but it wouldn't give rise to spunk stains on your sheets."

"There aren't any spunk stains, I always use my handkerchief," said Horace indignantly and then he clapped his hand to his mouth for he realised that he'd given the game away!

' "Now, now, don't be a silly boy, there's nothing wrong at all with taking yourself in hand once in a while," I said soothingly and lifted up the eiderdown to look for myself at what this ecclesiastical gentleman had to offer. I was pleasantly surprised to see a fine-looking specimen hanging over his thigh, while resting on the sheet below his shaft lay a very heavy pair of balls. I passed my tongue hungrily over my lips for it had been three days since I had any canoodling. Goldhill had been busy seeing to Polly as usual and my boy friend Jack the blacksmith's son had been laid up with influenza. So I took off my blouse and skirt and sat down on the bed clad only in my chemise.

' "My child, what in the name of heaven are you doing?" stammered the Reverend Horace Dumpole.

' "I thought you might like to hear my confession. I've got quite a few juicy stories to get off my chests," I said.

' "Surely you mean *chest*," he corrected me.

' "Oh no, chests, both of them," I chuckled, quickly slipping off the chemise and pressing my bare bubbies together which made him gasp. His trouser snake began to stir under the bedclothes. "Would you like to hear my confession or not?" I demanded, climbing up on top of him.

' "I would love to, my dear, but you see I am not a Catholic," he said regretfully.

' "Well, neither am I but you can still listen to

them if you like!" I said, as teasingly I dangled my breasts up and down his body, just grazing his skin with my tawny titties. Moving down, I could see his erect cock throbbing with excitement so I lowered my nipples on to his knob and just brushed it. I knew he wouldn't last long and I only had to repeat this three more times before he shot an immense white fountain of sperm up over his belly. His cock twitched so powerfully that a few flying drops of spunk caught me on my breasts. Oooh, this did make me feel randy especially as I let my titties slide in the little pools of jism on his tummy. I lifted my nips up and licked up the sticky cream as best I could.'

Of course, by now, Frank and I both sported capital stiffstanders and Sally took hold of them in her hands as she continued: 'He was a nice chap, old Horace, and after what I have just told you about he always left me half a crown on the bedside table each morning as a tip for bringing in his early morning tea to his room.'

'And of course, for his daily wank!' I commented.

'Oh no, Master Rupert, I didn't rub his prick every day,' said Sally.

'You didn't?'

'No, occasionally I would suck him off!' she chuckled. 'He gave me a ten shilling note for that [*fifty pence or about eighty cents – Editor*] which I thought was very generous. On his last morning when I came in he had already taken his bath and was sitting on the bed in his undershorts. He must have been thinking about me because I could see the purple knob of his prick had reared up above the waistband of his drawers. I set

116

down my tray and without a word undressed until I stood naked except for my chemise. With trembling hands he pulled down the shoulder straps and caressed my titties until my pussey was as moist as anything. I pulled off his shorts and his stiff veiny shaft sprang free and I kissed the uncapped helmet whilst fondling his huge balls.

'He leaned forward and kissed my neck and he lifted me across to the dressing table. I sat on it and opened my legs and buried his face between my unresisting thighs. He sucked up all the love juice that was trickling down from my cunney and then his tongue found its way further until it found my clitty. He chewed on it which almost sent me off then and there but with a groan he carried me back to the bed and I lay on my back, my swollen sex lips waiting for his swollen tool. He groaned and then thrust his shaft straight in my cunt without the least difficulty. His heavy ballsack slapped against my wet bum as I wrapped my legs until he spurted his juicy froth inside me in a marvellous mutual spend.'

'That was surely worth more than ten bob,' said Frank, panting slightly as Sally was now wanking both our cocks by rubbing our shafts against the soft velvety skin of her inner arms.

'You're right there, Master Frank, he pressed a pound note into my hand after we had both dressed,' she said complacently.

'You must be quite a wealthy young miss,' I said laughingly.

'Not really,' said Sally. 'I enjoy sucking and fucking but would never do it just for money. I wouldn't even have taken the presents Horace and other gentleman have given me but I'm

117

helping my brother Tom through college. He won the Sir Louis Baum Scholarship to Oxford University last year. But he always needs money for his living expenses and there are so many books that he has to buy.'

'What is he studying?' I said, breathing in heavily as Sally had now changed her style to tossing us off more slowly by making a circle with her forefinger and thumb and rubbing up and down the length of our cocks, barely touching the skin but chafing deliciously against the ridges of our knobs.

'He's taking a degree in Politics, Philosophy and Economics. Tom's a fervent Socialist and wants to become a Member of Parliament.'

'Never mind about those members, here's a member which is about to spout cock juice!' interrupted Frank as my own prick started to jerk uncontrollably in Sally's hand. We spunked almost together and Sally leaned forward to lick one cock and then the other, licking and lapping the jism that flew out of our bursting shafts.

Alas, we did not have time to repay the compliment though both of us would have appreciated a lesson in muff-diving from the gorgeous girl. But, hopefully, this would come at a later time. 'By the by, Master Rupert,' said Sally as she walked to the door. 'I couldn't help reading that lovely poem you wrote to Miss Wigmore which I saw in your exercise book. Now I don't want any money from you or Master Frank but I'd be very happy if you wrote a few verses for me to put in my scrapbook. Would you do that for me?'

As I said just before, you simply cannot keep anything secret from the servants! I should have reported her to Mr Goldhill for looking in my bedside drawer, but she had more than repaid this trifling wrongdoing! And her request for a keepsake was hardly a bothersome imposition.

'Very well, Sally, Frank and I will spend the morning composing an ode to you, on the condition that you don't show it to all and sundry in the servants' hall downstairs,' I said with a grin.

'I promise I won't, Master Rupert, never fear,' she replied as she opened the door. 'Shall I tell your Dad that you'll be down for breakfast in half an hour? You know how shirty he gets if you aren't at the table by half past eight and it's nearly twenty past eight already!'

Sally was right about my father's mood when Frank and I finally came down to breakfast. 'What sort of time do you call this?' he demanded. 'Young Folkestone, I'm sure your house has finished breakfast at this late hour.' Frank nodded weakly as he helped himself to tea and toast. 'Is that all you're having? There's bacon, eggs, sausages, kedgeree [*an Edwardian breakfast favourite of cooked flaked fish, rice and hard-boiled eggs – Editor*] and Mrs Randall will cook you a steak if that takes your fancy.'

'No thank you very much, sir, I rarely eat a cooked breakfast,' replied Frank politely.

'H'rumph, well, you must keep your strength up,' remarked my father and I muttered to my chum that he could have said that at least one portion of his anatomy was being kept up without any problem! My mother, who had been perusing the *Manchester Guardian*, looked up and said: 'Have you two boys forgotten that Mr Nolan is making a film this morning? He left a message to

119

say that if you are interested in seeing him at work he has gone to Knaresborough Castle. Your father has provided him with a horse and cart and he left here about an hour ago.'

Great Scott! In all the excitement of our late night and early morning escapades I had forgotten all about our American film-maker. 'Fred Nolan's a damned fine horseman,' grunted my father. 'I offered him the choice of a motor vehicle or the services of one of our coachmen but he declined, saying that he preferred to take the reins himself. But then he spent a year down in Texas as a cowboy so I suppose that's where he became such an expert.'

'Can we ride over there?' I asked.

'Certainly not, it's only two miles and you're best to hike it. I daresay you can travel back with Mr Nolan but a brisk morning constitutional will do you good. You both look a bit pasty round the gills this morning. Mind, I don't know why either of you should both look so tired, neither of you took any exercise yesterday.'

Little did he know!

CHAPTER FOUR

Captured On Camera

FREDERICK NOLAN WAS A FORTUNATE MAN, because the fickle English climate decided to greet our visitor from America with a morning of brilliant summer sunshine. Not even a hint of cloud could be seen in the morning sky as Frank and I trudged up the high road to Burbeck Field, whence Mr Nolan had been directed by my parents. Although the walk was not of a great distance, most of the journey was uphill, for Knaresborough stands on the summit of a hill overlooking the River Nidd. When we reached the outskirts it was easy to see why Mr Nolan had been recommended to use this location, for the luxuriant woods by which the little town is surrounded, the winding river at its foot, the venerable cottages, placed tier above tier on the face of the rock, the ruined castle and the old church combine to make up a most beautiful picture.

'Take the footpath just a hundred yards up the road on our right and Burbeck Field is behind the grove of silver birch trees you can see from here,' I said to Frank as we marched up Knaresborough

Road. 'The field itself is private land owned by Diana Wigmore's father. It is marvellously shielded by the trees, so one has a glorious view of the castle with the benefit of almost complete privacy.'

We made our way through the trees and we soon saw our horse and trap. Standing in his shirtsleeves behind a camera set up on a tripod was Mr Nolan and in front of the camera was none other than Katie Harbottle, dressed or rather undressed in a flowing white gown through which one could clearly see the curved outlines of her figure. She was standing in a classical stance, with one leg moved slightly forward and with her arms outstretched arms, a pose which pressed her breasts against the fine covering and her nipples showed up darkly through the finely spun cotton where her breasts bulged against the almost transparent material. Frank and I exchanged a knowing glance – so this was how Mr Nolan made moving pictures of the beauties of Yorkshire!

Surprisingly, the couple did not seem embarrassed in the least by our presence. In fact, Mr Nolan greeted us with a hearty 'Hi, fellows, what's been keeping you? Katie and I have been here for nearly two hours already.' He went on to explain that he wanted to make the first *tableau vivant* movie [tableaux vivants *were common in late Victorian years. In these shows actresses dressed in body stockings or even in the nude, could pose in dramatic classical or historical scenes on the strict condition that they never moved. The ban on nudity in the British theatre, except for bare-breasted girls who had to remain stock still, was not lifted until the*

*abolishment of stage censorship in the late 1960s –
Editor*].

'Shall we rehearse once more, Fred?' suggested
Kate. 'It will certainly help to have an audience.
Although you tell me I must always look at the
camera, if the boys stand with you, I can see
whether they are enjoying my performance.'

'Great idea, kid,' he replied, diving behind a
black cloth and making the final adjustments to
the focus mechanism. 'Try it one more time and
then we'll commit you to immortality on
celluloid. I need the strong sunlight for a
satisfactory exposure. You see, the showmen are
becoming more fussy and won't now accept dark
prints.'

'What do you mean by that, Mr Nolan?' asked
Frank. 'Who are these showmen you mention?'

'I'll tell you later,' he promised. 'Okay, Katie,
let's try it one more time.'

On his command Kate swirled around, dancing
nimbly around the relatively small area of the
field which was in the range of Mr Nolan's
camera. Then she slowed down to stand just six
feet away from us and teasingly, tantalisingly let
slip her robe to stand stark naked in front of us.
What a voluptuous beauty was Kate and how we
drank in the delights of her nudity. Her face was
finely formed with dark silky hair falling down in
curved ringlets onto her shoulders. Her breasts
were luxuriantly large, hard and firm, as white as
snow and tipped with delicately small nipples,
that were already raised like two pink bullets.

What a perfect picture of female pulchitrude
she made! We stood gaping whilst Fred Nolan
reloaded his camera and Katie let her hands fall to

brush her nipples softly and then passed them upwards to turn through her hair. The movement made her breasts lift and the flushed circles of her aureoles which ran around each nipple heightened in colour, framing the juicy tittie at the centre as if they were bulls' eyes on target boards.

Frank and I were not alone in wriggling uncomfortably as our erect cocks battered against the material of our trousers. Frederick Nolan, however, was already one step ahead and was busy tugging off his braces. 'Now look here, Rupert,' said the American moving picture pioneer hurriedly, as he sat down to remove his shoes and socks.

He ripped open his shirt and continued: 'Here's the chance of a lifetime for you to make moving picture history! I've put a new magazine of film in the camera and I want you to come over here and keep the camera pointing at the action whilst you wind this handle at a steady pace. Like this, do you understand? Now, Frank, you hold the camera steady and point the apparatus forward if Rupert asks you to when he will have to point the lens to the ground. When we begin filming, look at your watch – you have a second hand on it don't you? Good, now three minutes after Rupert begins turning the handle you call "cut". Rupert then knows we have come to the end of the picture, so I will reload the camera. Get it? Good boys, I know you won't let me down.'

We were still somewhat dazed by the rapid-fire instructions but we took up our positions as the movie-maker rapidly completed undressing and ran over naked to the trap, pulling out a yellow blanket which he brought back for Katie to stand on. His swollen penis stood up high against his stomach like a marble column and Katie gasped with satisfaction as she arched her hips forward to feel the proud throbbing against her flesh. She was almost the same height as Mr Nolan but she bent her knees slightly so that she could experience the delicious feel of his hard prick more directly against her pussey. She tilted her head to receive his mouth upon her full, red lips. He pulled away for a second to shout: 'Start, rolling, Rupert!' before he returned his attention to Katie and covered her mouth with a burning kiss.

I cranked the camera as Fred caressed the silky smoothness of Katie's back, his hands stroking deeply into her shoulders and down along her spine. Katie began to lean away from him, drawing him down on to the blanket and Fred lowered his body on top of hers with one of his legs dangling between her thighs. Then he heaved himself up to sit across her thighs, his legs gripping her hips as he cupped her quivering breasts with his hands, letting his fingers trace patterns across them as he gently tweaked the ripe strawberry nipples that were now as erect as could be.

Frank had moved the camera as directed and I concentrated on catching the expression on Katie's face as Fred moved the tip of his upwardly curved diamond hard cock towards her mouth. She opened her lips to receive the purple-domed crown and took hold of his pulsating penis in a firm yet tender embrace, looking admiringly at the delicately blue-veined rigid shaft before moving her mouth along it, lapping, licking, sucking, moving faster and faster as her hands now clasped his tightening hairy ballsack.

'Not so fast, young lady, not so fast,' growled Nolan who realised that he was in danger of releasing his sperm too quickly under this exquisite palating of his prick. 'I don't want to spend before we have to change the film.' So he took out his gleaming staff from her mouth and laid it between the firm swell of her breasts. Katie lay back and I let the camera focus upon her soft white belly and upon the mossy tuft of curly black hair between her legs and the superbly chiselled crack with its pouting lips which she parted with her fingers to reveal the glistening red gash of her cunney. 'Lick my pussey out, Fred,' she asked the American. He smiled his assent as he athletically sprang up and took up a new position, kneeling in front of her parted thighs.

'Cut!' yelled Frank and, momentarily startled, the couple looked towards us. 'Oh well, we could have found ourselves just beginning the paradise stroke,' sighed Mr Nolan, as he heaved himself up to effect the necessary mechanics. It took only a few moments and I waited until he was back between Katie's legs before shouting: 'Ready when you are!' and began to display what turned out to be his considerable pussey-eating talents for the camera.

I have kept a copy of this film in a locked compartment in my secretaire ever since and I understand that Dr Radlett Horne, the aptly named specialist in sexual dysfunction, also possesses a print of Mr Nolan paying attention to Katie Harbottle's pussey which he screens to patients and students alike as a perfect example of how to perform cunnilingus.

Mr Nolan started by letting his tongue travel down the length of her velvety body, stopping briefly to lick around her navel before sliding down to her thighs. He was still kneeling when he parted the crisp curls of her thatch to reveal her damp, inviting cunney lips which opened like a lust-hungry mouth, eager to welcome the tip of Fred's questing tongue. He worked his face down into the cleft between her thighs. Even through the viewfinder of my camera. I could not help but notice how appealing her pussey looked. Doubtless Fred Nolan was even further stimulated by the delicate aroma of cunney juice that had already drifted across towards Frank and myself.

Now he was down on his belly, between Katie's legs with one hand under her gorgeous backside to provide additional elevation and the other reaching around her thigh so that he was able to spread her pussey lips with his thumb and middle finger. She began to purr with pleasure as he then placed his lips over her swollen clitty and sucked it into his mouth, where the tip of his tongue began to explore it from all directions. Katie became very excited and thrashed about as he increased the vibrations of his tongue, wrenching out little yelps of excitement from the trembling girl who was now near to coming off. She wrapped her strong thighs around him and buried his head in her bush as he slurped noisily, varying the sensations for his partner by taking time out to lick the insides of her labia, kissing and sucking until her pussey must have been a veritable sea of lubricity.

'Aaah, that is heavenly! More! More! Oh Fred,

you've sent me off!' cried Katie as she twisted and turned whilst her paramour sucked up the flow of love juice as she shuddered into a body-wracking orgasm.

Mr Nolan scrambled up to lie on top of Katie and he slipped his hands around her back to clutch the plump cheeks of her warm bottom. He chuckled and said: 'I'm so pleased that I was able to bring you off with my tongue. Sucking off can be hard work for a man but it's so gratifying when the girl achieves a spend. But now, Katie, I am going to fuck you. Would you like to know just how?'

'Oh yes, please, do tell me.'

'Well, first I shall mount you and then I'll decide just how we will take our pleasure. But for now, I'm going to lie upon your belly and inset my long, thick cock into your wet little snatch. Then I'll feel the velvety clinging muscles of your cunney as I move my shaft in and out of your juicy cunt – and we'll see what happens from there.'

He moved surprisingly quickly, smoothing his hands over her breasts again which sent her into fresh raptures of delight. Then he was on top of her, hungrily searching for her mouth as they exchanged a burning kiss, moving their thighs together until their pubic muffs were rubbing roughly against each other. Fred's stiff prick probed the entrance to Katie's exquisitely formed crack and he lifted himself up on his hands and knees so that I was able to obtain a marvellous close-up shot of his swollen knob forcing its way through her pussey lips into the squelchy wetness of her cunney.

Like a steel bolt, his cock rode thickly through the moist channel, separating the folds of gluey skin and fucking higher and higher, only pausing when it was prevented from further progress by the jamming together of their loins.

'What a wonderfully juicy cunt,' panted Fred, as his body rose up and down, thrusting his sinewy shaft in and out of her yielding vagina. 'Katie, I do believe that you'd fuck day and night if you could.'

'Oh yes, yes, yes. Fuck me, Fred, fuck me – no more talking, just ram that big tadger faster, oooh, that's the way!' she gasped in reply.

Her eyes were shining and moist and a beautiful colour bloomed in her cheeks – such a shame that this could not be captured on celluloid, I thought, cranking away until Frank suddenly shouted: 'Cut, we're running out of time.' Alas, this meant that Mr Nolan had to scramble up, his erect cock glistening with cunney juice, and change the film once again before rushing back to place his prick back in its moist, warm haven of Katie's cunt.

'I'm ready when you are,' I called out and he took up where he had been forced to leave off. He moved his hands around her gorgeous curves with practised ease, squeezing her firm breasts, rubbing the big red stalks of her nipples against his palms as she took hold of his magnificently gleaming stiffstander and guided it back into her yearning cunney. Katie wrapped her arms and legs around Mr Nolan's lithe frame and urged him to make it 'hard and fast, Fred – I want to feel every inch of your big fat cock when you spunk into me.' She clamped her feet round his back and drummed her heels against his spine as he pounded his penis into her soaking little nookie. She took up the rhythm of his thrustings and this was too much for poor Frank. He let go the camera and tearing off his trousers, started to wank his enormous prick, frigging it up to bursting point.

'Join in, join in!' cried Katie, so he shuffled over to them, his trousers round his ankles, his cock in his hand. She took hold of his pulsing tool and pulled his knob into her mouth, lashing it with her tongue as she sucked noisily away. Frank shot a fierce jet of love juice between her lips just as Fred drenched her eager cunney with a flood of frothy sperm as Katie's hands clasped his bum cheeks, pushing him deeper and deeper inside her as she brought herself off into a tremendous spend.

'More! More! More!' she cried out, desperate to prolong the grandeur of her fulfilment. Gamely, Fred drove on and I could see the copious quantities of spunk overflowing from Katie's cunt and running down the crevice of her bum. One last spasm wracked their bodies and they fell back exhausted though Katie still had the strength to suck up the last remaining milky drops of Frank's sperm from the 'eye' on his now softening helmet.

'M'm, that was a splendid coupling, gentlemen,' said Katie, as she recovered her senses. 'Dear Fred, you really are one of the best fucks I've ever had, and Frank, dear boy, what a delicious *bonne bouche* your sweet cock made during it all.'

Fred smiled his thanks. 'Thank you, Katie, and

may I truthfully say to you that for me that you have one of the most magnificent cunnies it has ever been my pleasure to encounter. My prick will ever be at your service whenever you require it.'

After the participants had dressed themselves, Mr Nolan carefully put away the exposed film which we would have developed at Ramsay's Studios near Paddington Station in London. I still have a good copy of the print and often amuse myself and occasionally house guests these days by showing them this erotic little moving picture.

[*Alas, no copies of this film have survived. An interesting aside here is not just that Rupert Mountjoy acted as cameraman on the first ever British blue movie. For this was not the first European sex film – this honour goes to* Le Tub, *a movie made a year earlier in 1897 by the French pioneer Georges Meliès using the newly developed techniques of the Lumiere brothers – Editor.*]

But then, to my discomforture, I heard the unmistakeable sounds of the rustle of clothes behind us. I turned my head and to my horror saw that we had been joined by the Reverend Campbell Armstrong, a curate from Farnham, a little village close by, and Barbara, the second daughter of Major Dartland, the Squire of Farnham, a man of choleric disposition who my mother detested because of his antediluvian political views that would not have disgraced Ghengis Khan!

For how long had they been watching us? Oh well, I would just have to brazen it out ... 'Good morning, Rupert,' said Reverend Armstrong in his soft Scottish burr. 'Is the weather not glorious?

Ah, I believe you are acquainted with Miss Dartland.'

'Good morning, Reverend,' I replied. 'May I introduce Miss Katie Harbottle of Harbottle Hall near Wharton? This gentleman is Mr Frederick Nolan from the United States of America and this is Frank Folkestone, my best chum who is staying with me during the holidays.'

He beamed a bright smile at us. 'So pleased to meet you good people. I am Reverend Armstrong of Farnham and this is Miss Barbara Dartland whose father is the Squire of our little community.'

'Good morning,' said Barbara shyly. 'Mr Nolan, are you the owner of this moving picture camera?'

'I am indeed,' said our American guest. 'Would you care for me to explain the workings of the machine?'

Barbara smile. 'Oh no, that won't be necessary, for I was shown such a camera by my Uncle William whilst he worked with Mr Edison in your country.'

'Your Uncle William – good heavens, you don't mean Will Dickson, by any chance? But what a coincidence! He and I are the greatest of friends. Why, I was one of those who advised him to leave Mr Edison three years ago and join Biograph. He is a great pioneer of our industry.'

[*W.K.L. Dickson was indeed a truly important player in the production of the first moving pictures. He worked with Edison and then moved to the inventor's great rivals Biograph in 1895 and constructed a very different kind of camera which avoided Edison's patents. He helped build the first Biograph studio which was*

132

situated on the roof of the Hackett-Carhart Building on
Broadway in New York City – for the only real source of
power for the early film-makers was the sun! – Editor.]

'I could not help observing that you were filming your actors *au naturel*,' said Reverend Armstrong genially. 'Was this an educational film, perhaps, for students?'

'You could say that,' agreed Mr Nolan, as I looked more closely at Barbara who I had only seen a handful of times before on formal occasions. She was an attractive girl of perhaps twenty years, somewhat sallow of complexion with dark brown hair over a rather low forehead but with a most pleasing expression of face. Even at this early stage in my career as a cocksman, it occurred to me that her large sparkling eyes promised sultry pleasures and it was not too long before I was proved right in this assumption.

After a few minutes conversation, Barbara said: 'Why don't you join us for a drink before luncheon? We have brought an ice-box with us. Campbell, perhaps you would be kind enough to bring the pony and trap over here?'

'With pleasure,' replied the young Scottish cleric and he walked off to fulfil her request. Barbara confided to us that Campbell was a terribly sweet young man. 'It is just as well that my Papa doesn't know that Campbell is one of those clergymen who hold progressive views, or he would forbid me to see him,' she confided.

'So I presume that Campbell has no objection to the consumption of alcoholic beverages,' commented Katie Harbottle.

'Certainly not, and being of Scottish stock, you will not be very surprised when I tell you at times he can be a liberal imbiber,' replied Barbara with a slightly furrowed brow.

'But something troubles you, I can see,' Katie continued.

'Well yes, and seeing your film was very appropriate in the circumstances. You see, although Campbell may drink, he does not fuck.'

'Does not fuck!' gasped Katie in horrified astonishment. 'Surely such a masculine-looking young man is not of the persuasion favoured by Oscar Wilde?'

'Oh no, Campbell is no homosexualist. Indeed, he would very much like to fuck me but his religious belief forbids him to do so. I would not mind so much – for I respect his sincere religious conviction – but he really does not know how to pet properly and so I don't even get to enjoy a good kiss and cuddle.'

'This is bad news, but I have an idea,' said Katie. 'Let's all have a drink first and I'll tell you what I have in mind later.'

Campbell returned with the pony and trap and Fred helped him bring down the ice box and a large hamper. 'Why do cooks always provide enough food for an army?' he asked good-humouredly. 'It is uncanny how they know we will share our meal with friends.' How true, I thought, for we were almost in the exactly same situation I had found myself a few days before with Diana Wigmore.

Barbara was spot on target about her ecclesiastical friend's indulgent attitude to the two bottles of chilled white wine. Frank and I preferred lemonade but Campbell, Fred, Katie and Barbara had no problem in polishing off the

Chablis by themselves.

After our *al fresco* luncheon, Fred, Frank and Campbell decided to take a short stroll in the woods. I decided to remain with the two girls and lay in the long grass, using my jacket and rucksack as a pillow. Although my eyes were closed I could easily overhear the conversation between Katie and Barbara and their heart-to-heart chat certainly made my young prick stiffen up pretty smartish!

Barbara began it all by saying: 'I do envy you, you know, Katie dear, for you seem to have achieved total liberation if your love-making just now is anything to go by. If only I could enjoy such freedom, for not only my parents but also my gentleman admirers are so fuddy-duddy in their thinking that I do believe I shall go quite mad if I have to exist in this state for very much longer.

'It isn't so much my Papa, who is known for his old-fashioned obstinacy but dear Campbell who causes me such grief. I mean, he is so inhibited! We have exchanged kisses, many quite passionate and I have seen the swelling outline of his cock straining against his trousers. I have even brushed my hand against it once as if by accident of course, but the dear boy is so backwards in coming forward that I despair of his ever even caressing my breasts whilst we are engaged in an amorous embrace.'

'My dear Barbara! How extraordinary! It appears to me that you have a quite beautiful pair of bubbies. Any lad worth his salt would give his right arm to cup them in his hands and squeeze them,' said a shocked Katie.

'Thank you, Katie, I would have thought so –

my previous beaus have always tried as soon as possible to unbutton my blouse and caress my bare breasts. Oh Katie, I would like nothing better than to have Campbell's hands on my naked nipples. But he has never plucked up the courage to go further than a passionate kiss although I have now managed to make him put his tongue inside my mouth! I think he is frightened that he will upset me if he takes further liberties. You see, I am a virgin and do not feel ready just yet to enjoy the fullest delights of sexual play but I really would like to experience the joys of petting. I would greatly value your advice on just how to proceed as I feel very frustrated.'

'I'm hardly surprised to hear that,' said Katie kindly. 'Frankly, I am just astonished that any man could fail to be overwhelmingly aroused by your feminine charms. However, if I were you I should sit Campbell down somewhere and tell him before your lips touch his that he need not fear to let his feelings show, because you do not wish to let matters progress to their natural conclusion. Now, I do not believe for a moment that Campbell would turn out to be a cad, but just in case he does become over-excited once you begin the proceedings, I would keep a glass of cold water handy. I have found that either thrown in the face or down into the lap, a glass of cold water proves an ideal weapon against a too-ardent suitor.

'It's extremely doubtful that you will need any such protection with Campbell. Mind, he may become a different man once you have stroked his cock – men do, you know! Mind, I do not think that prick-teasing is a suitable sport for a lady. Once you begin you must continue until he obtains relief one way or the other through ejaculation, either with your hand or with your mouth.

'But first things first; come over here and sit next to me. Now let's pretend that I am Campbell and we are about to kiss.' Obediently, Barbara moved over to sit down next to her companion. Katie wrapped her arms around her and murmured: 'Now I think what would happen next is that he would take off your blouse once you had put your tongue inside his mouth.'

And through my half-shut eyes, for I was still feigning slumber, I saw the wicked little minx unbutton Barbara's blouse and opened her chemise to reveal an absolutely delightful pair of soft rounded globes, each tipped with large aureoles and hard, pointed nipples which Katie immediately covered with her hands. 'Is that nice?' enquired Katie as she found the opening to the other girl's skirt and quickly unleashed it so that Barbara was clad solely in white frilly knickers and stockings.

Whether by accident or design, I am unsure, but Barbara's legs were already slightly parted when Katie's hand slyly insinuated itself between them and began to rub her mound through the semi-transparent material of her drawers.

I only feasted my eyes on this lascivious scene for a moment because Barbara let out a little scream, saying that she could see the others returning from their walk in the woods. Reluctantly, Katie said: 'Oh, then put on your skirt and blouse but leave the top buttons undone so Campbell can see the swell of your lovely breasts. Gosh, he is a lucky man! If I were he, I would nibble upon your luscious red titties and bring you off by frigging your juicy cunney.'

'Katie! How could you be so rude!' said Barbara reprovingly but from her tone of voice I could see that she was not really offended by Katie's blunt country speech. She had plenty of time to prepare herself by the time the men returned and I stretched my limbs and let out a huge yawn as if I had just woken up from a deep sleep. When the others reached us Fred Nolan announced that he would be taking his camera to a picturesque location they had discovered during their walk.

'Come on, Rupert, we'll take the pony and trap,' said Frank.

'Do you mind if I stay here, I've got rather a headache coming on and I'm going to sleep it off,' I fibbed, and Campbell and Barbara also demurred.

'As you like,' said Fred Nolan. 'We'll be back in about an hour and half.'

As they left, I rolled over and pretended to go back to sleep, leaving Campbell and Barbara together nearby. Sure enough, as soon as the coast was clear, they fell to kissing and cuddling in the most passionate fashion. Yet Campbell forbore to let his hands move towards Barbara's bosoms even though she had left the top buttons of her blouse invitingly open as Katie had instructed. There was only one way forward, she must have thought, for she took hold of Campbell's hands herself and cupped them firmly around her magnificent breasts.

'Don't you like my titties?' she asked plaintively.

'Oh yes, yes,' he groaned, 'but I fear that if I let my hands stay there they might be tempted to stray elsewhere!'

'Don't fret about it, I would have no objection,' she told him as she opened the remaining buttons of her blouse. Even this highly disciplined young clergyman could not be unmoved by the sight of her bare breasts as she shrugged off the garment and opened her chemise. Her dark hair, now fully undone and hanging in long tresses, veiled yet highlighted her firm, bouncy breasts. The swell of those superb orbs acted as magnets to Campbell's hands as he squeezed the milky white globes and let his fingers play with the tawny, taut nipples which had risen up to greet him.

This stimulated the pretty girl so much that she let her hand run down to his lap from which bulged an alarming protuberance. As their lips crashed together once more she opened the buttons of his trousers and out sprang his huge stiffstander, sturdily rising upwards. Barbara took hold of his swollen shaft and I must say that this holy son of Hibernia had been blessed with an enormous prick. It stood up, blue veined and as stiff as a board, jutting out at a slight curve. Barbara pulled back his foreskin and exposed the giant bulbous knob. She started to rub her hand up and down the giant staff but this set Campbell off into a wild frenzy. He almost ripped off Barbara's knickers in a frenzy of lustful desire and her thickly matted brown triangle of pussey hair came into view, with the little pink labia already fluttering out in anticipation of the joys to come. He then pushed her legs apart and separated her cunney lips with a questioning forefinger, letting it run up and down the full length of her exquisitely fashioned crack.

'Ooooh, Ooooh! Oh, Campbell, at last!' panted Barbara, as the curate continued to let his finger slide along the edges of her pouting slit. 'Now work it in and out of my cunt, there's a dear man.' He looked shocked at her frank words but as they engaged in yet another almost bruising kiss, he let one and then two fingers dip in and out of Barbara's honeypot. She purred with pure lust as she continued to rub his prick up to a stupendous height whilst by now Campbell was sucking and slurping away on one enlarged brown nipple and flicking and teasing the other between his fingers at a great speed. When Barbara reached down and handled his balls, the curate's body visibly shook and a fountain of sticky white cream spurted out from his cock. Barbara was by now trembling with the force of her own orgasm which rippled through her just as the last dribblings of spunk oozed out of Campbell's cock. In her delight she bent forward and lapped up the last dregs of his spend and the curate looked shocked. But she simply smacked her lips and said: 'There's nothing wrong in swallowing sperm, Campbell. I do so enjoy the salty taste of spunk. It is the most invigorating of tonics and it enables me to remain a virgin whilst bringing us both to the summit of the mountain of love. And come to think of it, I am making sure that you are guiltless of the sin of Onan who let his seed fall upon the ground. [*See Genesis 38:9 – Editor*.]

Campbell was not without a sense of humour and he said: 'I'm not too sure about the theology, my love, but the main reason is good enough for

140

me. What a pity though that you only managed to lick up a morsel.'

'Ah, well I'm sure we can see if the well has not dried up,' said Barbara, dropping to her knees and taking the now shrunken helmet of his prick in her hands. She stroked his soft, hairy ballsack and took his entire limp shaft into her mouth, rolling it around her tongue until in a very few moments she took it out the transformed tool, now hard as rock again! She kissed the top of this massive red topped truncheon and sucked lustily on the uncapped ruby crown. Barbara had to stretch her jaw to cram in Campbell's big stiffie and continued to lick and lap away whilst frigging his shaft which brought on his climax very quickly. With a throaty moan, he shuddered and the first creamy jet of spunk came hurtling out of his cock. The first jet hit Barbara's nose but then she opened her mouth wide and gobbled furiously upon her sweetmeat, swallowing quickly to keep pace with his tangy libation. Then, as his spend passed its peak she took his entire shaft back into her mouth, sucking for all she was worth to extract the very last milky drops of love juice from his pumping prick.

As they lay together, exhausted by their frenetic passions, I would have given anything for the opportunity to give myself some much-needed hand relief. But the lewd pair were looking almost directly at me and I could hardly move or they might guess that I had been watching them all the time!

Barbara was the first to stir from their reverie. 'Campbell, did you enjoy yourself? I'm ready for more larks if you are.'

'I'd like to carry on but though the spirit is willing, the flesh is weak,' he sighed ruefully, flipping his limp penis with his hand.

Barbara looked sorrowfully down at his turgid cock and said: 'Never mind, you don't need a stiff prick to release a lady. How would you like to kiss my pussey? I'd really be happy if you would. Have you ever done it before?'

He blushed and replied: 'Back in Dundee there was a wee lassie named Lizzie who liked to have her cunney kissed. I'm not sure though that I was any good at it as she used to say that only my friend Eddie could bring her off with his mouth.'

'I'd like to find out for myself,' said Barbara, looking around to ensure that they were still alone. She unbuttoned her skirt and wriggled out of her knickers. She smoothed her hand between her parted thighs, letting her long fingers run through the thick tuft of curly brown hair through which I could just about see her cunney lips poking invitingly through their hirsute covering.

The curate heaved himself up to kneel before her and I could see that though there was now a crimson flush of excitement on his face, his prick still dangled flaccidly between his legs. Gingerly, he bent his head forward and planted a chaste kiss on her hairy mound. Then he kissed her furry bush again, this time with more feeling, and then again and again until he rained a veritable deluge of kisses upon her cunney. Now he was lying on his belly, his mouth tightly affixed to Barbara's pussey which, though hidden from my view, must have responded to his attentions. Very soon Campbell was sucking and slurping her love juices with uninhibited abandon. This set Barbara

142

off, for she clamped her legs around his head as he paid court to her cunt whilst his hands reached up and grabbed her breasts, rolling her titties around in a circular motion. I heard Barbara breathe: 'Oh yes, finger-fuck me, darling,' as Campbell continued to pleasure her pussey as her hips moved up and down with increasing vigour until finally, with a convulsive tremor, she shouted out with great passion and came off, drenching his face with her love juices as she writhed in the delicious agonies of her orgasm.

'Was that good for you?' enquired Campbell somewhat unnecessarily as he raised himself up on his knees.

'Lovely, that was really lovely,' she sighed. 'Campbell, you tongue pussey beautifully and though I have yet to experience it, I cannot believe that your cock could be a very much more powerful organ. I adored the way you began with a light flicking motion on my clitty and then how you switched to cover the length of my crack from the clitty to the arse-hole. Oh darling, I so want you to make love to me!'

He looked down and I saw that his once-turgid cock had now stiffened up into an enormous erection that poked up between his thighs like a flagpole. 'I would give anything to fuck you, Barbara, my sweet, and I fear that if we continue to carry on this way, this will happen as surely as night follows the day.'

'Then let us do it! I am tired of the stealthy hidden kisses, the furtive fondlings and clandestine meetings,' she declared, holding his throbbing tool and pressing it to the cleft between her gorgeous breasts. And who knows, perhaps

Barbara would have lost her virginity then and there if the sound of the pony and trap had not been heard in the distance. They hastily broke away from each other and dressed themselves in record time so that all was seemly by the time Fred Nolan stepped down from the driving board and said cheerfully: 'Hello there, you two! The sun has gone behind the clouds so until it reappears we thought we would come back and keep you company.'

Campbell smiled weakly and I am sure that Barbara would have been lost for words but I saved the situation by giving a loud yawn and saying: 'Ah, what a difference forty winks can make. My headache has totally vanished and I'm quite fit again. What shall we do now?'

'Alas, I must be off as I promised to chair a meeting in the village hall this afternoon,' said Campbell. 'Actually, it's of the local Sports Club. Er, I don't suppose you would care to join us, Mr Nolan. Yours is such a fascinating profession that I am sure the members would be greatly interested in anything you had to day.'

'Members are usually more interested in which pussies they can slide into,' muttered Frank quietly as Fred Nolan shook his head.

'Thank you for the invitation but I must be getting back and start developing my film which will keep me busy for some time. Katie, boys, would you like to stay here or go back to Albion Towers with me?

'Oh do stay,' begged Barbara. 'These meetings can be tedious but they don't last too long and then if you have time we can go back to my house for tea and crumpets. I can always arrange for

Connor to take you back in one of our carriages.'

No doubt because Mr Nolan would be busy in the darkroom, Katie promptly accepted her invitation but Frank decided to go back home with Fred Nolan as he genuinely did feel the beginnings of a headache coming upon him (in later life poor Frank – or Sir Frank Folkestone to give my oldest friend his proper present-day nomenclature, for he inherited the family baronetcy in April 1912 when his father perished at sea, being a passenger on the ill-fated *Titanic* – has suffered badly from severe migraines, the pains of which can only be mitigated by lying down in a darkened room and when possible, having his prick sucked by a willing naked maidservant though I doubt whether his physician prescribed this latter treatment!).

'What a shame! After we have concluded the few items of business our little gathering is to be addressed by the hypnotist Dr Glanville Porterfield and it could prove to be a very interesting affair as he will offer to hypnotise members of the audience,' she said with regret.

'Oh, I'd like to come and see Dr Porterfield in action, if I may,' I piped up.

'Certainly, Rupert, do join us,' said Campbell and so I asked Frank to instruct Goldhill to send Wallace our coachman back with the pony and trap to Farnham Village Hall at five o'clock sharp. 'Katie, Wallace can take you back to Harbottle Hall,' I added.

So we made our way to Farnham Village Hall where fifty or so ladies and gentlemen of the local gentry were gathered. The main business of the meeting was to thank those ladies and gentlemen who had taken part in the croquet, cricket and

145

lawn tennis matches played by Farnham against other localities.

Most of these matters were only of minimal interest but I will record the words of one Mr Anthony Cheetham, the captain of Farnham cricket team, which so far that season had vanquished all before them, winning eight matches and drawing one, and that only because rain stopped play when Farnham were poised for victory. He asked that despite past successes all members of the side should keep their noses to the grindstone. Mr Cheetham's wise advice was reproduced later in the week by our county newspaper and, being a keen cricketer myself, I reproduce them here – American readers of my journal may well consider that they apply equally to baseball, a sport which I also enjoy in the summer months. He said: 'It is related of the Hon. Peter Forbes-Hornby, one of the best-known old Yorkshire gentlemen sportsmen, that whenever he had an unoccupied half hour, he used to set up a stump and bowl at it. It is to be wished that there was more of this commendable practice. Bowling is much more of dogged perseverance than of initial skill and many more players would stand a chance of distinguishing themselves by their bowling than by their batting.' Mr Forbes-Hornby also said: 'A good cricketer will always keep a ball perpetually about him; to be always tossing it and throwing it so as to get thoroughly used to the feel of it.'

Perhaps this is how Mr Forbes-Hornby achieved his sensational throw of more than one hundred and twenty yards with the cricket ball which was witnessed and attested to by Mr Cheetham though it was impossible to ascertain the distance with absolute accuracy for the ball struck the trunk of a tree some four feet from the ground.

Once all these affairs had been completed, we settled down to listen to Dr Porterfield's address. He began by explaining just what hypnotism is – an artificially induced state of semi-consciousness characterised by a greatly increased susceptability to suggestions made by the hypnotist. 'There is nothing supernatural involved despite the warnings of some ignorant and irresponsible journalists in the popular press,' said Dr Porterfield, a plump, distinguished-looking gentleman who, though almost as bald as a coot, nevertheless sported a full black beard. 'Although the science of hypnotism probably dates back to ancient times, it was the Austrian physician Friedrich Mesmer [(1734-1815) – Editor] who first used hypnosis in a medical capacity, proving that by imposing his will upon that of his subject, he could treat his patients and at the same time spare them much pain.

'On the music hall stage, there are hypnotists who put members of the audience in a trance and make them perform strange acts. Frankly, this concerns me as I believe that hypnotism is a serious business and should not be popularised purely for the purposes of amusement.'

His speech was interrupted by a snort of disapproval from a lady sitting in the back row. The Reverend Armstrong, acting as Chairman, frowned and cleared his throat as he stood up, presumably to ask for order, but Dr Porterfield waved his hand. 'No, my dear sir, I think it obvious that the lady at the back has a point to make. Madam, would you like to say something?'

The lady concerned rose to her feet. She was a not unattractive woman in her early thirties, with a haughty expression on her rather sharp features. 'That's Mrs Robinson. She's a real martinet of the same ilk as my Papa,' whispered Barbara to us.

'I don't believe a word of all this mumbo-jumbo,' said Mrs Robinson firmly. 'I'd like to see somebody try and hypnotise *me*!'

'Well, rest assured, Madam, it is extremely difficult for even the most expert practitioner to hypnotise somebody against their will,' said Dr Porterfield.

'Stuff and nonsense! That's just an excuse – I've seen a so-called hypnotist at work at a house-party and he pretended to make a gentleman believe he was a duck and go quacking all round the room. He made a lady say "Please do not touch my nose" to another lady five minutes to the second after she came out of her trance and performed other parlour tricks.'

Dr Porterfield spread out his hands. 'These may have been parlour tricks, but I assure you that if the hypnotist was genuine then these tricks, as you term them, were genuine enough and had not been planned beforehand by those concerned.'

'I find that hard to accept and would need further proof,' she said, shaking her head in disbelief.

'Then come up to the front and I will hypnotise you here and now,' said Dr Porterfield. 'On the condition that you will not fight against me, I will prove to you and the ladies and gentlemen present, that I am not trying to perpetrate a gigantic confidence trick.'

'Very well,' said Mrs Robinson and made her way up to the stage to an excited buzz in the audience. Campbell Armstrong gave her his chair and she sat down, looking directly at Dr Porterfield. He called for silence and then took out his pocket watch and dangled it on its chain in front of her.

'Just look at this watch,' he said, 'and follow its progress as it moves from side to side. There, you are feeling sleepy, very sleepy. Your eyes are drooping and now, on the count of three, you will be asleep, one, two, *three!*'

The audience watched fascinated as Mrs Robinson's eyes closed as she sat slumbering in her chair. 'Raise your right arm,' commanded the hypnotist and she immediately obeyed. 'Now when I tell you to do so, you will try and rest your elbow on your lap. But your arm is so light, as light as a balloon so though you want to bring it down, you find you cannot do so because it flies up again straightaway. Now, on the count of three, try to bring down your arm, one, two, *three!*' It was quite extraordinary how Mrs Robinson dropped her arm and that as soon as she did so, it shot up again as if of its own accord!

'Are your subjects able to speak under hypnosis?' asked Katie Harbottle.

'Oh yes,' said Dr Porterfield and, turning to Mrs Robinson, told her to open her eyes. 'Now perhaps you will tell us if you received any visitors at home earlier today?'

An innocent enough question to be sure – but what a Pandora's Box was opened when Mrs

Robinson replied that her friend Mrs Thatcher had come round for morning coffee. 'Oh, yes,' said Dr Porterfield. 'And what did you talk about?'

Mrs Robinson replied: 'We had a most exciting conversation about Walsh, the new window cleaner who has taken over from Chamberlain who moved to Alwoodley last month. Walsh is a most personable young man and does his work far better than his predecessor.'

'He makes the windows shine brighter?' prompted the hypnotist.

'Never mind the bloody windows,' she said impatiently. 'It's his prick that Mrs Thatcher and I were concerned about.'

'His *what*?' spluttered Dr Porterfield, who was as shocked as anyone in the hall.

'His prick,' she repeated. 'After all, Chamberlain was hardly up to completing his round any more, what with trying to satisfy up to a dozen ladies who wanted to be fucked during one working day. But I think Walsh will be able to cope. He came round yesterday afternoon and after he'd done his work he came into the drawing room –'

'Stop her, Dr Porterfield, tell her to stop talking!' said Campbell Armstrong urgently, pulling Dr Porterfield's coat-tails to attract his attention. But the unfortunate hypnotist's foot slipped as he turned back again to instruct Mrs Robinson to keep quiet – though by now the cat was well and truly out of the bag – and he crashed over Reverend Armstrong's chair sending them both sprawling onto the floor. Although the curate was only slightly dazed by the impact, our poor speaker hit his head on the floor with a resounding crack and was as soundly out for the count as if a pugilist had felled him with an uppercut.

Barbara Dartland, who had undergone a first aid training course, frantically applied a cold compress to Dr Porterfield's head to revive him but, like the vast majority of the audience, I was far more interested in the revelations of Mrs Robinson!

She was well on her way telling us what she had told Mrs Thatcher what Walsh the window cleaner had been up to after she had rewarded him with a glass of beer for cleaning her windows. 'He said to me: "Mrs Robinson, I've always considered you to be a beautiful woman and you have one of the shapeliest figures in the village." As I listened to his shameless flattery, sitting snugly beside him on the sofa, he slipped his right hand into my blouse, under my chemise and began gently squeezing my breast. I raised my hand as if to stop him but my nipple already had swollen up to the size and hardness of a little red pebble. Yes, I know that I should really have stopped him right there but between you and me, my dear Margaret, I liked the look of this muscular young man! He then wormed his hand between my thighs and as we french kissed, he worked them into the leg of my knickers and touched the moistening lips of my pussey. My juices began to flow freely as my thighs tightened like a vice over his hand as I shuddered to a little spend as his fingers penetrated me.

'Then the naughty fellow began kissing my neck and throat and I suggested that we retire upstairs to a bedroom. He helped me undress down to my drawers and I lay back on the bed as he kissed my titties and my belly before rolling me over and kissing and licking me all the way back to my shoulders. My poor pussey was now sopping wet as he peeled off my knickers, kissing each inch of exposed flesh and he ran his hand lightly down the crack of my bum before rolling me back. He plunged his tongue inside my ear and then played the tip around my titties before his mouth travelled down to lightly bite the insides of my thighs. Then he drove me wild by licking and lapping at my dripping cunney and I was already on my way to paradise even before he found my clitty. He brought me off in style before I told him I wanted his prick inside me.

'Then he pulled off his shirt and undid his belt and let his trousers fall to the ground. Teasingly he told me to take off his pants so I carefully pulled them down over his hard, stiff cock. It wasn't that huge but his shaft looked well proportioned enough for a good fuck so, pulling back the foreskin, I rolled my tongue over his purple knob and sucked it right into my mouth. It tasted wonderful!' This fully released my passion and I gobbled his cock until I felt it throb with desire. I released him so that he could climb between my legs and place his rigid rod inside my pussey. It stretched me nicely and I pulled my knees as far apart as possible to allow him to give me his full length. He fucked me beautifully with firm, pumping strokes, not too quickly, giving me the full benefit of his sinewy prick before shooting a huge jet of jism into my cunt as I squirmed my way to a tremendous spend.

'We clung to each other whilst he recovered but his cock was still semi-stiff when it slid out of my cunney. He raised himself up to his knees and the cheeky rogue placed his prick near my face. I reached out to hold the glistening shaft which was still wet from my juices and I decided to work him up to another full hard-on. I teased the knob by running the tip of my tongue all around the ridges of his helmet and then gave the underside a few quick licks and that did the trick, stiffening up his tool right back to its former firmness. I took his whole knob into my mouth and then eased in the rest of his stalwart staff. I bobbed my head up and down on his cock – three short, licking sucks followed by one long, fierce sucking was enough to send him off. The lusty lad was so excited by all this that in no time at all I felt his succulent cock shoving hard against the back of my throat and his hot, salty spunk was released and I felt it flooding down my throat. Walsh has got quite enormous balls, by the way, but by swallowing convulsively I drank every last drop of his copious emission, milking his tool of every last drop of the liquid of love.

'I managed to stiffen up his cock for one more fuck but then he had to leave as he was already late for Mrs Humphries and she wanted some special servicing too!' concluded Mrs Robinson. God knows what else she might have said but fortunately Barbara had by now revived Dr Porterfield and he quickly snapped the lady out of her trance. The audience had been stunned into silence, though one or two youths at the back had sniggered occasionally during her telling of this lascivious tale.

153

'There you are, I told you it was all hocus pocus,' said Mrs Robinson with satisfaction. 'I'd better be going now as I forgot to pay Mr Walsh the window cleaner yesterday and I'm expecting him back at the house.'

This brought forth howls of laughter but, quite undaunted, Mrs Robinson made her way to the exit. Reverend Armstrong stepped forth and, after explaining to Dr Porterfield what had occurred, called for silence: 'Ladies and gentlemen, I trust that what we heard this afternoon will never be revealed. Indeed, I am going to swear every person here to total secrecy. I will brook no exceptions, and Dr Porterfield agrees with me that, ethically, Mrs Robinson's words should be treated in the confidence she would have expected during a medical examination or, if she were of the Catholic faith, in the confessional. Would everyone please raise their rights hands and repeat after me an oath that we will never speak of what we heard just now. If there is anyone who has the slightest doubt about the justice of this, then I would remind him or her that Walsh is unmarried whilst Mrs Robinson's husband is a military man who is often away from home. Poor Mrs Humphries, as we all know, is a young widow. So only he that is without sin should cast the first stone.'

(Let me state here that I only mention the incident now in written form fourteen years after the event because Walsh married Mrs Humphries in 1904 and the couple promptly emigrated to New Zealand. Mrs Robinson and her husband, alas, perished along with Frank's father on the ill-fated maiden voyage of the *Titanic*).

We all went back to Barbara's house afterwards

for tea and, to everyone's relief, her parents were out for the afternoon. Reverend Armstrong said that he had some matters to attend to and would join us later.

Barbara insisted on opening a bottle of champagne from a case that an old French friend of her family had recently sent over to them, and the sparkling bubbly wine certainly loosened our tongues. It seemed to make Barbara and Katie forget that I was present for the presence of a young lad did not inhibit them in the slightest in discussing matters of the utmost privacy and intimacy in front of me. For example, after discussing Mrs Robinson's hypnotic confessions, Katie said: 'You know, it was interesting that a member of the working class such as Walsh the window cleaner had the finesse needed to make a good fuck great. After all, many men from the very cream of Society do not understand the subtle nuances of fucking, especially those who are well hung and who know it. Oh yes, they know that we can be excited by seeing a nude man with a flaccid cock, if his knob hangs over his balls.

'But simply just sticking your big shaft into a wet pussey isn't enough – after all, *anybody* can do that if he has the equipment for it. No, once a man gets a hard-on, I like a little foreplay like having him hover over me and rubbing his erect prick up and down over my breasts and belly and then finally on my clitty whilst he tells me how beautiful my breasts are or how juicy my pussey is and how much he loves my body. That will start me off and then I like him to begin inserting his shaft in my cunt, just a little at a time. First his

155

helmet goes in and then when he pulls it out the feeling of the ridge rubbing against my pussey lips is simply divine. Fred Nolan is very good at foreplay, by the way. Once he starts fucking in this style he puts his hard shaft in just a little further each time and the tension builds up deliciously. I find this much more exciting than just having every inch of a cock inserted immediately. Mind, even after a good fuck, I am often still usually highly charged and it is really super if my lover licks my cunney or manipulates my clitty with his hand after he has spent because that will make me come or give me a second orgasm if I've spent already.

'What is really dreadful is if he just rolls over once he's finished and doesn't even kiss or hold you afterwards. And I hate it when a man says "Did you come?" If I have, he'll know it and if not, well, we can always try again. But when he asks me I have the feeling that what he's really trying to do is asking me to rate his love-making abilities, which is unnecessary. Simultaneous spending is over-rated anyway, in my humble opinion.'

'You are really knowledgeable about *l'art de faire l'amour*, Katie,' sighed Barbara. 'As I said before earlier today, I do so admire your adventurous spirit. Here am I who have yet to experience the joy of feeling a prick up my cunt. Mind, I must confess that I am not totally without experience. For instance, I did have a very strange evening with a girl named Lizzie Hollywood the other week which led to my cunney playing host to other fingers than my own and, come to think of it, something else besides a strange hand!

'But let me first tell you about Lizzie. She is a pretty girl of about our age who I met for the first time at an exhibition of English Post-Impressionist art at the Manor Hall Gallery in Leeds. The wealthy textile magnate, Sir Louis Segal, donated some works from his collection and I met Lizzie at a reception given by Sir Louis for supporters of the gallery (my Mama has been a patron for many years). We got to talking and she told me she was an art student. As I was on my own – I was staying the night with my old friend Angela Bickler and I had the keys to her house – I accepted Lizzie's invitation to dine with her at the Queens Hotel. We drank a bottle of wine with our splendid meal and what with the aperitifs we had consumed at Sir Louis's party, I was feeling more than slightly woozy by the time we had finished our desserts. "Come upstairs and lie down on my bed for a bit before you leave. Give me your friend Angela's address and I will ask the reception desk to send word to her and inform her that she should not wait up for you," suggested Lizzie and, taking my hand, led me to the elevator. It seemed like a good idea at the time. I certainly had imbibed not wisely but too well for I collapsed on the bed and in an instant was deep in the arms of Morpheus.

'I woke up a couple of hours later and for a few moments I was totally disorientated and wondered dizzily where on earth I was! Then I suddenly remembered as I looked at my wrist-watch, for the bedside light was still burning and I saw that it would soon be midnight. I shivered as I felt a cool breeze blowing through the half open window. I raised myself up to shut it and it was only then when I looked in the long wall mirror that I suddenly realised that I was stark naked! I looked wildly around for my clothes when Lizzie came in from the bathroom. She was only wearing a cream silk nightrobe through which I could see the dark protuberances of her nipples as she walked towards me.

' "Ah, you've woken up at last!" she smiled. "Do you feel better now?"

' "Yes, thank you, I feel fine and dandy after that rest. I am so ashamed though, falling asleep after dinner but I'm afraid the bottle of Château Mouton-Rothschild went straight to my head," I stammered in reply.

'She came and sat by me and stroked my hair. "It doesn't matter at all, it really doesn't. I hope you don't mind but the night air is so warm and you looked so uncomfortable that I undressed you whilst you were sleeping. I've hung your clothes up in my cupboard and before you worry your pretty little head about it, I've also let Angela Bickler know that you're staying the night here and that you'll contact her first thing in the morning."

'She then slipped off her robe and lay down next to me. "You don't mind if I join you, Babs, as I'm feeling rather tired too," she murmured, snuggling up close to me. Lizzie was really a very attractive girl with long blonde hair that she let down to fall over her shoulders, whilst her light complexion and slender figure contrasted so well with my own rather dark looks. She moistened her rich red lips with her tongue, showing her sparkling white teeth. Her legs were next to mine and I must admit that our figures complemented each other perfectly, even our pussies blended so well, mine brown-haired and curly, hers silky and blonde.

' "You still look tired," Lizzie said softly. "Why don't you put your head on my shoulders and close your eyes?" I readily complied, feeling totally relaxed and though Lizzie was soon stroking my sides and fondling my breasts in a most intimate fashion, I made only the slightest token attempt to stop her. "What are you doing, Lizzie? That's very naughty, you know," I admonished her drowsily.

' "Just relax my love and let me pay court to your beautiful breasts – aren't they large? They are so much bigger than mine," she cooed and I offered no resistance as she continued to caress my bosoms, cradling them in her hands. I closed my eyes as I felt Lizzie's lips close upon my right nipple and swirled it in her mouth, sending chills of desire running up and down my spine. She moved her hands up and down my body now in smooth, gentle titillating strokes and to my own surprise I found myself growing more and more aroused with each caress. As her knowing fingers inched towards my pussey I felt my thighs stiffen and my hips involuntarily thrust forward in tantalising anticipation of what was to come.

'She slid her long fingers into my dampening muff, moving them deliciously inside as the heel of her hand rubbed my clitty which rose up to greet it until it was as hard as a tiny walnut. "Ah, I've found your secret spot, have I not?" she whispered as she drew firm little circles around my clitty until my entire body was squirming with pleasure. Without ever taking her fingers from my clitty, she brought across her other hand and dipped a long

159

forefinger in my squelchy hole. The sensation was so electrifying that I sat bolt upright and moaned: "Oh Lizzie, that's wonderful!"

' "It's wonderful for me too, darling. Finger fucking your cunney makes me so wet," she breathed into my ear. "Feel my pussey, it's positively dripping waiting for your touch." Without protest I let her take my hand and place it between her cool, firm thighs. I trailed my fingers through her silky blonde cunney hair and we covered each other's mouths with burning kisses as we finger fucked each other's cunnies. Lizzie then moved her head down and nuzzled her red lips around my curly brown bush. "Darling, what a perfectly delicious crack you have! M'mmm, and what a stimulating, heady perfume it possesses!"

'Without further words she started to tongue my crack, moving all along my wet slit, exploring, tasting, teasing – and then suddenly she stopped! I gasped out my disappointment but Lizzie said sweetly: "Don't worry, sweetheart. I have a surprise for you." She reached out into the drawer of the bedside table and pulled out a strange black rubber dildo.

'Obviously, my surprise must have shown on my face for Lizzie said: "Barbara, have you never seen a ladies' comforter before?" "Oh yes," I said, still looking curiously at this strangely shaped instrument, "but never one like this."

' "Ah, this will be your first experience with a double-header – I promise that you will find it most exciting. One part of this dildo has been modelled upon the prick of the famous Shakespearean actor Mr Michael Beattie and the other is fashioned from a plaster cast of the gallant prick of none other than Lieutenant Colonel Alan Brooke of the Hussars, perhaps the most famous cocksman in England."

'Without further ado she took out a small jar of pomade and poured some of the sticky oil over the dildo which she then pressed gently against my cunney lips as she continued to nibble around my pussey with her mouth. This made me so wet that she was able to work the dildo head (I believe it was the slightly less thick end which had been manufactured to the measurements of Colonel Brooke) into my cunt until it filled me completely.

'Lizzie then pulled herself up until she was sitting upon my thighs. Our eyes locked as she finger fucked herself with one hand whilst she vibrated this rubber prick inside my cunt with the other. When her cunney was nice and juicy enough she then raised herself up and slowly worked the other part of our rubber playmate into her cunney. She reached forward and pulled me to her until we were pressed tightly together, breast to breast and cunt to cunt with the dildo pleasuring us both at the same time as we jerked our hips to and fro along its long double-headed shaft. I wrapped my legs tightly around her back and she wrapped hers around mine as, rocking back and forth, we achieved a delicious rhythm that sent pulses of pleasure to every nerve centre in my body.

'As our excitement grew, our motions became even more frenzied and Lizzie pressed me flat onto the bed and stretched her body out across mine, the dildo still clamped between our suctioning pussies. I grabbed her waist and pulled her towards me, allowing the rubber cock of Colonel Brooke to slide even further inside my sopping cunt. This was the closest I have ever been to a genuine fuck and I loved every glorious second of it.

'Suddenly my body convulsed and my head thrashed back and forth against the pillow. "Oh my God! Lizzie, don't stop now whatever you do! Lordy, that feels so great!" Of course Lizzie did not stop, and kept fucking my cunney as well as her own as she rocked to and fro. As soon as she felt me spend she felt the stirrings of her own approaching orgasm and we climbed the peaks almost together, shuddering and heaving as our cunnies poured out generous libations of love juice upon the sheets which were already stained by our perspiration and previous spendings.

'We lay there, drained and exhausted, pressed together still and joined at the crotch by the dildo which we took out carefully, first from my cunt and then from Lizzie's and she deposited it back on the table. We took a short nap but this time I was the first to wake and whilst she slept I caressed her as slowly and lovingly as she had earlier made love to me. I licked and nibbled at her small but proudly jutting breasts and her nipples rose to greet my mouth. I ran my palm down her belly and into her soaking blonde muff which woke her up and she smiled happily, closing her legs gently upon my hand.

'I ran my fingers through her silky triangle and my forefinger slipped easily into her sticky pussey which made her purr with pleasure. I had never gone down on another girl before (though several girls had done this to me at boarding school) but my curiousity and pervasive lust to which should be added to the desire to please Lizzie too were enough to overcome any slight resistance I might have felt towards the idea. So I slid down between her slender long legs and clasped my hands around Lizzie's boyish, rounded bum cheeks. I separated them as she arched her back to bring her tangy cunney up towards my mouth. I licked and lapped around those savoury cunt lips, moist from both our juices and then sucked her clitty into my mouth. This made Lizzie thresh around under me and with each of her writhings I felt my own pussey spend a little. I managed to straddle her leg so that I was able to feel her knee against my clitty. We made love again and each time Lizzie moved passionately her legs pressed more heavily against my cunt. As my excitement rose even higher I sucked up her cunney juices with renewed vigour. Finally, her whimpers and groans gave way to one long full-throated scream and we came together for a second time in a total, blinding release. We lay there together in bed before falling asleep for the night in each other's arms.'

I was worried that my prick might literally burst out of my trousers for I had been inadvertently been playing pocket billiards throughout the recounting of this outrageous history. I wiggled about uncomfortably but my shaft remained as stiff as iron when Katie declared: 'You'll be ready soon enough to have Campbell or whoever you so desire poke you. Do insist that he stays the whole night with you, though, when you finally do decide to take the plunge. I adore it when my lover makes love to me in the morning after a good night's fucking. For example, quite recently I was fucked by Mr Harry Barr, the gossip columnist of *The Pink 'Un*, a sporting paper which wanted an interview with my Papa about his stable of racehorses. Mr Barr was a competent enough lover though nothing amazingly special as far as technique goes. But on the morning after we made love, I opened my eyes and found him licking out my cunney. Now I vaguely recall something pleasant about a dream I was having but I didn't connect it with what was actually taking place. I was dreaming that I was out on Scarborough beach when I saw a piece of wood carved in the shape of a huge black prick lying in the sand. I got up and took off my bathing costume and eased the piece of wood inside my cunt.

'Then I woke up and found Harry Barr deep inside me and he told me, as he pumped his prick in and out of my juicy wetness, that he had been playing with my pussey for at least ten minutes beforehand, being careful not to wake me up. This was most considerate of him in the circumstances as his cock must have been straining at the leash. We then enjoyed a truly superb fuck, much better than the night before, and I suppose it was the bridge between fantasy and reality that made the experience so memorable for us both.'

As she finished her recollection, Katie looked across to me and with a saucy grin, said: 'This has hardly been suitable conversation for young Rupert to hear – mind, from the look of that bulge between his legs, I don't think it has done him any permanent damage.'

Barbara blushed but Katie's blood was up from the recounting of the stirring adventures – almost as much as mine! 'Come here, you naughty boy and let me see what you have hidden away in your trousers,' she called. 'Is that a catapult you have hidden in your pocket or were you simply stimulated by hearing the private confessions of two young ladies? Come sir, don't be shy.'

I walked towards them awkwardly, trying to conceal my bulging prick. But as soon as I was in reach, Katie swiftly unhooked my belt and ripping open my fly buttons, brought out my naked stiff cock into the sunlight. 'Isn't he well developed for a lad of his age?' remarked Barbara. I looked gratefully at her for I was used to only Frank receiving such compliments about the size of his shaft!

'Oh yes, indeed! I think that a good boy like Rupert – with an enormous prick that looks desperate for relief – needs to be attended to immediately,' said Katie, pulling down my trousers and underpants as she knelt in front of me. She took my cock in her warm, soft hands which instantly caused it to twitch delightedly whilst Barbara joined her and cupped my balls with one hand whilst gently rubbing her fingers down the length of my staff.

'With respect, dear Barbara, I saw it first,' said Katie as she opened her mouth and took my uncapped helmet between her rich red lips. The feeling was simple unbelievable as her darting tongue moved to and fro along the shaft. As she palated my prick I felt my balls swell under the caress of Barbara's hands and I thrust my shaft frenziedly in and out of Katie's mouth, knowing that I could hold back my spend for only a very short while. Barbara must also have guessed my urgency for she took my balls into her mouth and sucked them which caused a fierce rush of sperm to be sent shooting through the channel to the "eye" on the top of my pulsating knob. I exploded inside Katie's sweet mouth, flooding her throat with a deluge of sticky spunk which she greedily swallowed though she could not cope with my copious spend. My spunk gushed out between her lips and ran down her chin and finally fell upon Barbara's nose as she continued to suck my balls.

When Katie had finally milked my prick of its last drops of jism I stood there in a daze with my prick limp. Then Katie pulled Barbara aside and whispered something in her ear that I could not quite catch. Katie then turned back to me and said: 'We would like to see your cock stand up stiff again, Rupert. Can you oblige us?'

'Not yet, I'm afraid,' I said sadly looking down at my flaccid shaft.

'Well, I have the answer. Take off the rest of your clothes please,' she commanded and so I did just that, carefully putting them in a neat pile by my chair.

Katie grinned and said: 'Good – now we are going to play a little game. We're going to imagine that we are back at your school – St Lionel's, if I am not mistaken – and you have been summoned to the Headmaster's study for bad behaviour. Now sir, will you stiffen your prick!'

'I'm terribly sorry but I'm unable to just for the moment,' I mumbled.

'Very well,' said Katie crisply. 'Bend down, you

naughty boy, and touch your toes.' Again, I did as I was told, feeling rather nervous as Katie opened my legs slightly so that the girls could see my hairy ballsack hanging down. Then Barbara passed her hand lightly across my bare bottom cheeks and they began to wallop my arse with their palms, taking turns to smack me. It hurt a bit after a time but strangely enough did not feel as unpleasant as perhaps it should have done.

Smack, smack, SMACK! 'There, you naughty boy! How dare you visit us with a dangling tool!' Smack, smack, SMACK! 'Such an impudent fellow, isn't he? Take that, that and that!' I craned my head backwards and saw that whilst one girl was tanning my hide the other was busily undressing and by the time my arse was really stinging from their slaps, both girls were quite nude.

I looked down at my prick and saw that as if by magic it now stood up in a rampant state of erection, standing majestically high with the tip of my knob touching my navel. 'He's ready now,' cried Katie. 'Well, here's your chance, Barbara. I would let yourself be fucked by young Rupert, if I were you, so that when you and Campbell finally jump into bed you'll know exactly what to expect.'

'Do you think so?' said Barbara anxiously, as she thought for a moment before making up her mind. 'Yes, you're quite right, of course. Rupert, may I take it that you have no objections?'

My father had always drummed it in to my head that one should always help a lady in distress – not that I needed any encouragement as the lovely girl stretched herself out on the luxuriantly thick carpet. She really was an exceptional beauty with extremely large breasts topped by well-proportioned ruby nipples. Her mound was a veritable delight with a profusion of exquisite dark brown hair covering her furrow and the pouting lips of her cunney looked hugely inviting.

I knelt before this sensual goddess, spreading her legs wide as she grasped my rigid rod to feed it to her hungry pussey. She guided my knob between her cunney lips and slowly, thrillingly, I inched my staff inside her willing wet cunt as it sucked in my throbbing cock. I fucked her as slowly as possible, taking my time as her cunney muscles clutched sweetly at the sides of my shaft while I hovered above her, supporting myself on my arms. Then deeper and deeper, but still with deliberate speed, I thrust back and forth inside her. She began to moan and shudder and I paused. 'Am I hurting you?' I asked for this was after all Barbara's initiation into the grandest game, though her hymen must have been broken even before her tribadic double-ended dildo encounter with Lizzie with which we had just been regaled. I moved inexorably on, my hands holding her firmly just below her swaying breasts and I quickened my pumping at her request as I felt the walls of her love channel widen. She gyrated like a girl possessed and my cock was drawn in to the limit as I corked her cunt, my balls banging against her bottom as I plunged my prick in and out of her dark cavern.

The familiar tingle in my balls announced that the first surge of spunk was beginning its journey up to my rock-hard shaft. 'Can I spunk inside you?' I panted. Instinctively she opened her legs even wider, plumbing her hidden depths and as I drove in and out in the final passionate frenzy, her pussey exploded. She was wracked by great shudders that rippled through her body so that each time, however impossible it seemed to be, her cunney opened a little wider. As every current jolted through her she willed herself on, shouting: 'Yes! Yes! Shoot your spunk!' and she rose to meet me as I plunged yet again into her. The first unstoppable surge of sperm coursed its way up my cock. Time and time again I rammed into her, filling her cunt to overflowing with my jets of jism. Gush upon gush flowed into her from my spurting knob. My balls knocked unmercifully against her, throbbing with the mighty power of their emptying ejaculations.

A tide of relief washed over us as my pace slowed. Everything that was in me was now inside her cunt. The last irregular spasms of my come shook me and Barbara gave one last convulsive heave and then lay very still, her arms and legs splayed out, her breasts quivering still with the energy she had expended.

My lusty young cock was now truly spent and I pulled out my shrunken shaft and rolled off her. 'Well done, Rupert,' cried Katie, who had been following our coupling closely. 'I was most impressed that such a youthful prick could perform so well.'

'Well done indeed,' echoed Barbara. 'I came twice before you spunked. But I fear I have left little for you to enjoy, Katie. Poor Rupert will never manage another cockstand this afternoon.'

'Never mind, my sweet love; *carpe diem, guam*

minimum credula postero [*Seize the present day, trusting the morrow as little as you can – Editor*] and with respect to Rupert whose prick I would certainly enjoy having in my cunney or up my bum, I am well served for cock just now. If you recall, Mr Nolan the cinematographer has placed his Yankee pole at my disposal this evening and he really does know how to satisfy a girl.'

We decided to dress ourselves which was just as well because we had only just finished when the Reverend Armstrong arrived, to be followed shortly afterwards by Wallace in our best carriage. Katie accepted my offer of a ride back to her home as she wanted to leave Barbara and Campbell alone to enjoy themselves in privacy! I was feeling satisfied with the way I had spent the afternoon but on the way back Katie suddenly said to me: 'Rupert, would you think it amiss if I gave you a word of advice?'

'Not at all, Katie but I do hope that I have done nothing to offend you,' I replied in genuine concern, somewhat puzzled by the serious tone of her words.

She shook her head. 'Oh no, my dear boy, far from it. I would just like to say this to you. Fucking is the finest sport that a young man can engage in. However, if you ever reach the stage where one fuck is like another, when afterwards you cannot picture who it was you fucked and the particular taste of the girl concerned, then you should give your cock a rest and simply take yourself in hand – in every sense of the phrase if need be – until you are able to resume, refreshed and reinvigorated to enjoy the wonderful world of pussey and the ever-altering feel of one cunney from another.'

170

I pondered over her wise words. Over the years I have thanked the blessed providence for the fact that every pussey that I have ever encountered has been new and different in some way. Still, I have never forgotten Katie's counselling and there have indeed been periods – of as long as three or four weeks on occasion – when I have refrained from dipping my wick, even though the opportunity has been there for the taking.

At this early stage in my career as a cocksman, however, I simply filed Katie's warning in the banks of memory. I returned back to Albion Towers in the highest of spirits and naturally was eager to tell Frank about all my experiences.

'You should have come with me to Farnham, old chap, as I am sure that at worst, Katie Harbottle would have sucked you off even if she didn't want to fuck.'

'Not to worry,' said Frank cheerfully. 'I really did have a slight headache this afternoon and besides I had a jolly good time earlier on with Fred and Campbell whilst you were with Katie and Barbara.'

'Did you now,' I said, settling down in my chair as we idled away the time before dinner in the billiards room, undisturbed by any other members of the household.

'Yes,' he said smugly. 'I do not know whether it is the keen Yorkshire air that makes people so randy in this part of the world but I give you my word that I am not exaggerating a jot about what happened after luncheon. Fred, Campbell and I decided to trudge up to the ruins of Knaresborough Castle. Living so near, you must have been there many times, but Campbell told Fred

Nolan how the site of the castle commands prospects of great beauty and extent. Indeed, "Knaresborough From The Castle Hill" is a favourite subject with many artists.

'Campbell was telling us about a secret passage leading from the castle yard to the moat when we came across one of these artists, an extremely pretty lady in her mid twenties, sitting in front of an easel and looking earnestly at the scene in front of her. She was wearing a close-fitting costume in the modern style which showed off her slim body and lovely big breasts which jutted out like two melons. I don't mind telling you that my cock began to stiffen just at the sight of these two beauties which were only half hidden by a low-cut top.

'Well, what do ya know,' gasped Mr Nolan when we approached her. "It's Miss Patricia Miller or I'm a Dutchman. Hey, Patsy, how'ya doing, honey?"

'The girl looked up and, Christ, Rupert, she really was a beauty. Her mop of red hair set off the most beautiful face which lit up when she saw us. "My God, it's Fred Nolan," she cried out in a most pleasing Yankee drawl, "fancy seeing you here." They embraced each other heartily and Fred explained that Miss Miller was a distin- guished actress in her home town of Boston and had played in many of the top theatres throughout the United States. "Are you working over here, Patsy?" he asked and she shook her head. "I'm over here purely for a vacation, Fred. The London impressarios have been badgering me and I was tempted by a generous offer from Konrad Kochanski to appear in *As You Like It* at

Drury Lane in London. But I've turned him down along with all the others! I need to recharge my batteries and paint and sketch a little. I'm staying with Lord Hugh Hoffner at Hampsthwaite. Where are you residing, Fred? You really must come along to see me there, especially if you bring along your camera. His Lordship is fascinated by the idea of moving pictures.''

'Mr Nolan explained that he was staying at Albion Towers with your family, Rupert, and then after he introduced Reverend Armstrong and myself, Miss Miller showed us some of the pictures she had painted during her holiday. I looked over Mr Nolan's shoulder as he leafed through her portfolio but to my delighted surprise there were no landscapes of Knaresborough Castle or the surrounds – instead there were twenty or thirty sketches and most were precisely drawn studies of those parts of the human body that we rarely see on canvas! There were titties and arses, cunts and pricks galore, Rupert. My favourite was perhaps the one of a girl with her skirts thrown up and her naked bottom thrust out towards the beholder in such a fashion that, between the spread legs, one could see her furry auburn bush and her cunney lips that were already parted as if in eager anticipation of thrusting entry.'

'How fascinating! Isn't it the very deuce of a coincidence that only last week Diana Wigmore, another female artist who loves fucking, was good enough to rid me of my troublesome virginity. I'll tell you something, Frank old boy, even if I pass all the University examinations when we leave St Lionel's, blow Oxford and

Cambridge, I'm off to art school in London, Paris or Rome.'

My pal chuckled and continued: 'And I think I'll join you, although my brother Roger assures me that there is plenty of fucking available to undergraduates in both those august establishments. Anyhow, as I was telling you, Mr Nolan was also much taken by this drawing and demanded to know who the lady in question might be. "Oh no, I cannot tell you," said Miss Miller roguishly. "It would be wrong to divulge the name of my sitter, for all these drawings were done for private exhibition only. I mean, supposing I was to circulate a picture of your prick. I doubt whether you would want it bandied about amongst gatherings of strangers or passed from hand to hand even amongst those of your acquaintances. Don't you agree, Reverend Armstrong?"

'Campbell took her point and commented: "I agree that your lips should remain sealed, Miss Miller, and that we must think of your sketch only as The Unknown Cunt. However, the love-channel in question does appear to be a most welcoming furrow and one can hardly blame any gentleman for being curious to find out the name of its owner." He pulled out another drawing that showed a pretty, buxom looking young woman with a happy smile upon her lips about to kiss the uncapped knob of a well-sized erect prick that she was lovingly cradling in her hands.

' "Ah ha," said Campbell. "Now here is a sensitive sketch from life that I find most pleasing, with its suggestions both of vulnerability and of a half-ashamed boldness."

174

' "It does not offend you, Reverend?" twinkled the artist.

"Certainly not, my dear young lady," he quipped, "for it shows that the female in question has learned her catechism well. Does she not show that she knows what is the chief end of man? But I think you have based this picture upon an illustration from Mr Angus Gradegate's *Fucking For Fun* which must also be available in your country."

' "Well spotted," said Miss Miller with unconcealed admiration. "Only a very few people have ever made the connection."

Campbell replied modestly: "Well, I do have an unfair advantage here, as the girl who posed for the illustration in Mr Gradegate's valuable tome was my cousin Louise Lombert from Dumbarton and the member she is holding is that of her friend, Mr John Gibson of Edinburgh, a gentleman whose penis is reckoned to be perhaps the largest in all of Scotland."

' "Really now," said Miss Miller. "Is Mr Gibson still residing in Edinburgh? I plan to spend a few days there early next week and would appreciate an introduction." She turned to Mr Nolan and added: "You'll hardly credit it, Fred, but I've not had a good fuck since I came to England."

' "How terrible," said Mr Nolan as he took hold of the willing girl. "Let's put that right here and now! After all, we're old friends and I'm sure my companions will excuse me if I asked them to continue their stroll without me."

'Campbell whipped out a notebook and said that he would walk on to a park bench a quarter of a mile or so up the road. I would have joined him but the fiery-haired American girl said: "Don't leave us, young man. You may learn something to your advantage."

'Mr Nolan looked a little dubious but then his face cleared and he said to me: "Oh yes, I quite forgot, Patsy prefers an audience whilst fucking which I suppose comes from performing so much on the stage. Come on, let's go behind the clump of trees over there. After all, you're welcome to watch, Frank, but we don't want to admit the general public – especially as they would be able to see for free!"

'I followed the couple down the hill to the place Mr Nolan suggested and once we found an even piece of ground, I helped spread out the rug Miss Miller had brought with her and we laid it on the grass. Mr Nolan quickly stripped off and lay down on his back, his prick waving upwards like a huge, veiny truncheon. Miss Miller laughed gaily as she stepped out of her dress and slipped off her chemise. She wore no knickers (it was because the day was so warm, she later confided) and she paraded her naked charms which gave me a stiffstander in no time. What a ravishing sight she was, Rupert, and I almost spent there and then as her firm, thrusting breasts swung gracefully as she pirouetted lightly on the balls of her feet, letting me see her delectable figure. Straightaway I recognised her pussey from the picture that had so attracted us. "The Unknown Cunt", as Campbell had called it, was none other than a clever self-portrait for there in all its glory was the pouting little crack inside the curly auburn-haired triangle which nestled between her creamy white thighs.

'But I said nothing as she swooped down and washed Mr Nolan's knob with her tongue. She then wrapped her rich lips around the straining shaft and sucked lustily for a little before climbing up on him with her knees on either side of his torso. She pulled open her pink cunney lips and I saw her take hold of his cock and guide it inside her. Like Mr Nolan, Patsy Miller was an expert equestrian and this was shown as she rode his prick with great assurance, twisting her hips and bouncing merrily away, leaning forward so that he could take her cherry nipples in his mouth.

'Her face was now flushed with excitement and she turned to me and gasped: "Come on, let me see what you have to offer." I unbuttoned my trousers and presented my cock to her. She took it in her hands and peeled back my foreskin as she massaged my shaft. "Hey, big boy, what a whopper, that looks like a prick big enough for a man twice your age. And such a fine smooth-skinned shaft, as hard and stiff as anything, yet like velvet to the touch."

'She continued to bounce up and down Mr Nolan's prick as she leaned forward to lick and tongue my purple knob. Then, with a practised hand, she cupped my balls in the palm of her hand and gently pulled me towards her so that she could feed all of my shaft inside her mouth. Perhaps it was the lewd sight of Patsy sucking my cock which brought Mr Nolan off so quickly. "Are you ready for it, Patsy?" he panted as she rocked backwards and forwards on his prick in rhythm with the grand sucking to which she was treating my delighted member. I felt such delicious stabs of desire as she sucked my cock, teasing my helmet against the roof of her mouth with her tongue that I, too, soon felt the surge of a powerful spend coursing through my throbbing staff. We both spunked simultaneously and Mr Nolan filled her cunt with his copious emission of sticky white jism whilst I drenched her mouth with my spurtings of creamy sperm.

' "Thanks, boys, that was a nice brisk fuck. I really enjoyed that and I must tell you, Fred, that young Frank here has a lovely salty tang to his jism. M'mm, nothing tastes as clean and fresh as frothy spunk straight from the cock. My God, his prick is still stiff even after spunking! Oh well, let's not waste any time." She lay down on the sheet, and pulled me on top of her. I entered her easily, for her cunney was well greased from Fred's jism. I slid my full length deep into her and began to fuck her as she threw her legs around my waist. She arched upwards at every stroke, her bum cheeks coming off the sheet as she gyrated faster and faster. She wailed with ecstasy as I grabbed her breasts and brought my head down to suck those lovely red nipples. I felt her cunney contract around my cock as I thrust madly into her exquisite wetness and all too soon the sperm came bubbling up from my balls. Luckily, she reached port first, shivering and trembling as with one last push I started to spend, spurting my hot love juice inside her willing cunt. She gurgled with joy as my frothy white cream hurtled into her and she milked my prick superbly. Then Mr Nolan showed us his expertise at bum fucking and, as requested, I tossed myself off and squirted my sperm over her titties whilst her bottom hole was being flooded by Mr Nolan.

'So you see, Rupert, I didn't miss out too much by not joining you this afternoon at Farnham for I was absolutely shagged out and needed a rest!'

'You certainly did not,' I agreed and I asked him where Mr Nolan might be found. Frank informed me that our guest was still engaged in developing his film so I decided to go to my bedroom and take a bath as I was feeling hot and bothered after all that exercise at Farnham.

In my room, I took off my jacket when I suddenly remembered that our form had been set some holiday work by our English master Mr Bresslaw, the task being to write a poem of not less than twelve lines, a task which I had not yet completed. 'I wonder whether Frank has remembered either,' I muttered to myself as I took out the exercise book from my bedside drawer in which I had scribbled the verse to Diana which I have reproduced earlier in this narrative. Perhaps it was because we had been studying *Romeo and Juliet* and I had been much moved by the plight of the star-crossed lovers that I decided to try and pen some lines on the joyousness of love-making. I took off my jacket and sat down on my bed, willing the muse to assist me. The first few lines came quickly:

> *Tell me where are there such blisses*
> *When lips are joined in heavenly kisses*
> *When lovers both convulsive start*
> *The passion only love imparts*

Then, just as I was racking my brains thinking of how to continue, there was a demure knock on my door. 'Come in,' I called and Sally, our sensual servant, came in.

'What do you want, Sally, my room seems to have already been cleaned,' I said.

'I know, Master Rupert, it's been ready for you since noon,' said the blonde temptress. 'But Mr Goldhill told me to refill all the water jugs in the bedrooms – I'm sorry if I interrupted anything important.'

She set down the tray she was carrying with the jug on it and said: 'Are you writing another poem?'

I was shocked – how the devil did she know? As if reading my mind, she said: 'I read the verses you wrote to Miss Diana in that notebook. Well, don't be cross. You shouldn't have left it around if you didn't want anyone to see it. I'm good at rhyming, perhaps I can help you with your poem.'

Before I could reply, she was sitting besides me. To be honest, I did not believe for a moment that Sally would be able to complete my work. But I was wrong, dear reader, for Sally was blessed with an aptitude for versifying that put me to shame. It would bring a blush to all those of a reactionary disposition who insist that the labouring classes are incapable of anything but the most basic speech, thoughts and deeds. For Sally helped me greatly as I put together the following ode:

> Mutual keeping to one tether,
> Sweet it is to join together
> Throbbing, heaving,
> Never grieving;
> Thrusting, bursting,
> Sighing, dying!
> Decrepid age may beckon, teasing,
> Shrivelled up bodies we'll not abide,
> Vigorous youth, oh, that is pleasing,

It is worth the world beside.
Craving, wanting,
Sobbing, panting,
Throbbing, heaving,
Never grieving,
Thrusting, bursting,
Sighing, dying!

'Sally, you have hidden talents.' I laughed but she shrugged off what I now realise was an unintentionally patronising comment.

'Oh, we are quite capable downstairs of other things besides cleaning and cooking, you know. Mr Goldhill, for example, is a serious student of the art of ancient Greece and on his summer vacation last year went down to London to see the Elgin Marbles.' [*A group of fifth century BC Greek sculptures from the Athens Parthenon brought to England by the Earl of Elgin and now in the British Museum – Editor*]

'You surprise me, Sally, I suppose you'll tell me next that Wallace the coachman is a learned authority on the art of the Dutch masters.'

'No, Master Rupert,' she grinned. 'He doesn't even know much about Dutch caps. All that interests him is cricket, football, ale and fucking – which reminds me, as I've helped you with your homework, how about a farewell fuck before you go back to school?'

My eyes lit up. 'Now you're talking, Sally. Blow poetry and the Elgin Marbles.'

'Let me blow you instead!' she cried as she knelt before me and unbuttoned my trousers and peeled down my pants to allow my thickening bare cockshaft to emerge. My tool sprang out

181

eagerly from its squashed state, stiffening up quickly as she cupped my balls in one hand. Coyly playing with my truncheon with the other, sliding her fingers up and down the hot, sturdy shaft, first played with my prick, then gobbled almost the whole length of my shaft inside her mouth. Her tongue played lightly at the swollen uncapped helmet of my prick as she gently but insistently squeezed my throbbing balls. Her mouth sucked hungrily up and down my rigid rod, sliding her lips up and down my rock-hard shaft, gulping noisily as my knob smoothed its way across the roof of her mouth and down towards the back of her throat. I managed to unbutton her blouse and took her proud young breasts in my hands, flicking her titties between my fingers as I thrust my cock in and out of her mouth until very soon I pumped a stream of creamy spunk between her lips which she swallowed with the same sweet urgency with which we began this encounter.

Gad, is there anything more thrilling than having a pretty girl suck your cock? It adds that indefinable extra dimension to a good fuck best expressed perhaps by my old friend, Sir Loring Sayers, who commented in *The Cremorne* recently: 'Sucking a man's cock is the deepest, most sensitive way in which a woman can acknowledge her lover's masculinity.'

I am sure this was so with Sally, who now had me in thrall. 'Now it's your turn to taste me,' she said, quickly stripping off the rest of her clothes. She lay back on my bed and the sight of her exquisitely fashioned quim with the two pink cunney lips peeping delicately through the mass of blonde hair of her pussey simply carried me away. With a hoarse cry I leaped up to join her and parted her thighs even wider. In an instant I was licking and lapping her around her dripping treasure-trove. My tongue slipped deep inside her and I could feel her clitty swell as I probed even further. There was a refreshing tang of our mixed love juices as with a soft moan of pleasure she wrapped her thighs around my neck, forcing her splendid silky bush into my face.

I nipped at her clitty with the top of my tongue until she reached a delighted peak. 'I want you inside me,' she moaned, releasing my head from between her legs. I let her flop back on the bed, threshing and writhing in her own secret world of pleasure. When she had regained her composure she told me to lie on my back and she knelt over my prick which was still semi-erect. She brushed her perky titties over my knob, and this had the desired effect of making my shaft stand up to attention straightaway. She grasped my slippery shaft and rubbed it up and down until it was more than ready. Then she squatted over my twitching knob and guided it between her squishy cunney lips. My cock slid all the way up her sopping slit as I reached up to squeeze her creamy breasts.

Sally began to ride me with long steady movements of her supple thighs. I began to move with her and played with her luscious red-stalked titties whilst she rode me faster and faster. This was no slow, lingering fuck. We were both so urgent in our needs that with every thrust downwards upon my prick, I rose upwards to meet her with equal vigour. Great gasps shuddered through our bodies and the tingling in my cock became stronger and stronger and I felt that first gush of spunk forcing its way up from my bollocks. My prick twitched and I jetted my first wodges of cream as her cunney quivered all round my shaft and she began to spend with me. The muscular contractions of her cunt increased my pleasure even more and I shot a tremendous flow of sperm into her gorgeous love box as she fell forwards into my arms, shaking and yelping in delight as her pussey milked my pulsing prick of every drop of spunk.

We lay entwined, exhausted, sucking in great gulps of air. Neither of us could speak but she smiled up at me and puckered up her lips in a little kiss. Still inside her, I felt her cunney relax and I took out my now deflated cock. I looked sadly down at it but Sally said: 'Your tadger has worked very hard. I give him nine and a half marks out of ten which is half a mark more than I have ever awarded.'

'How about Mr Goldhill?' I asked.

'Oh, Stanley usually scores seven or eight but I've yet to give out a ten. Perhaps we'll see if you can hit the jackpot during the Christmas vacation,' she teased.

Now the flush that had suffused our bodies began to subside and we pulled on our clothes. I took my bath and changed and knocked on Frank's door. 'Frank, are you ready for dinner?' I called out. He came to the door, looking very spruce. 'That was well-timed,' he said. 'I've just said goodbye to Polly who came up to my room for a last fuck before I go home. I say, Rupert, this has been the jolliest vacation we've ever spent together, hasn't it?'

'We've certainly spent a lot, old chap.' I commented and we burst out laughing as we made our way downstairs to the dining room.

CHAPTER FIVE

Back To School

I HAVE ALWAYS LOOKED WITH PITY ON THE man who says that 'his schooldays were the happiest days of his life'. It is an undeniable fact that, when older men meet, they tend to hanker for the joys of youth, remembering the roistering of their salad days when they would besport themselves with wine, women and song. Yet whilst I enjoy ruminating over the fun of times gone by, it is not in my nature to sigh wistfully over past pleasures. I far prefer to look forward to the opportunities afforded by the future.

However, let me stress that I count myself extremely fortunate that my formative years were spent at St Lionel's Academy for the Sons of Gentlefolk, an educational establishment run on more liberal principles than the usual public school of its class. Great men have been scholars there and many sportsmen of renown have graced its playing fields. The majesty of the ancient grey buildings, set just south of the Ashdown Forest near the village of Maresfield, makes its pupils appear in their imagination to see themselves as heirs to a great tradition. Many, I regret to admit, were tempted to hold an unwarranted aloof sense of social superiority but Frank Folkestone and myself were amongst those who simply had a genuine love and pride for our old school.

In twos and threes we strolled along the tree-lined path leading to the Great Hall, exchanging greetings and comparing holiday notes with classmates we had not seen for several weeks. 'Should we tell them what we did on our holidays?' said Frank with a cheery grin as we entered Hall. 'They will all be so envious that I bet no-one will believe we now know the joys of fucking!'

I was about to reply when the deep, commanding voice of our headmaster Dr Keeleigh boomed out: 'Folkestone! Mountjoy! I would like to see you in my study at once.' Frank paled and muttered: 'Hells bells! How could the old bugger have heard me?'

'He couldn't have done, don't worry,' I reassured him but nevertheless I was still more than a mite worried as we followed the headmaster through to his large oak-panelled study. As the Bard of Avon has it, conscience makes cowards of us all!

In fact, of course, Dr Keeleigh had not heard a single word of Frank's lewd remark. We entered his study and the headmaster must have been reading my mind for he put an avuncular hand on my arm and said: 'Sit down, boys, sit down. Now I don't want to burden either of you this term as it is important that you work and play as hard as you can. The Fifth Form this year is of an exceptionally high calibre and knowing your fathers as I do, if either of you don't finish well up

187

the examination lists at the end of each term, I know you'll be for the high jump.'

We smiled weakly as the headmaster added: 'But I've every confidence in you chaps and feel that your shoulders are strong enough to carry a further burden. I want your help in a matter not only important for the school but also for our country.'

These dramatic words had us bolt upright in our chairs. What could Dr Keeleigh mean? He saw he had captured our rapt attention and continued: 'Tomorrow, gentlemen, a very special new pupil starts at St Lionel's. Now we are not talking about the usual case of an eleven-year-old boy who would begin his life here in the First Form. Firstly, this new chap is sixteen years old and will start his schooling in your year. Secondly, this new chap is an Indian. His name is Prince Salman and he is the eldest son of the Rajah of Lockshenstan, a land of vital strategic importance on the North West Frontier. The Prince's father is an important ally in our fight against the Afghan irregulars and those agents of other European powers who would like nothing better than to see our position on the Indian sub-continent destabled.

'I will let you boys into a confidence. Our government has persuaded the Rajah to let Salman be educated in the Mother Country. Previously he was educated privated by British tutors in the Rajah's palace so he speaks English perfectly. We have been honoured that on the advice of the Viceroy of India himself, the Rajah has chosen to send his son to St Lionel's. I would not be surprised if the Rajah knows of your father, Mountjoy. You lived in Delhi for some years as a young boy, if I remember rightly.

'What I want you boys to do for me is to take Prince Salman under your wing. He has been to England several times and so he will not find life here totally strange. Show him the ropes and keep him out of trouble. This should not pose too many problems because he is a studious boy and I am sure he will fit in well.'

'We'll be happy to help out, sir,' I said. 'May I ask a question though? What do we call him: Your Highness, Prince Salman or what?'

The headmaster beamed and said: 'An excellent question, Mountjoy. I think the best solution is that he should be known as "Prince" to staff and boys alike. He will be at the school just before luncheon tomorrow and I will call you up here as soon as he arrives. Any further questions?'

'No, sir!' we chorused and Dr Keeleigh waved us away. 'Good lads, I will rely on you. I've already informed the teaching staff about all this but you must feel free to speak to me in confidence about any problem that might arise.'

After tea, our form was ordered into a classroom to hear 'an important address' by the school chaplain, the Reverend Percy Clarke, the contents of which was known to us even before he marched into the room. Looking back, I think it probable that the Reverend Percy was himself a closet arse-bandit [*a common Edwardian term for a homosexual – Editor*] for he liked nothing better than to question boys about whether they ever had wet dreams, whether they ever fantasised about naked women, whether they had ever experienced erections and whether they ever

189

played with themselves. Of course, everyone denied everything (though in practice the true answer to any of his queries would have been in the affirmative for almost every boy!). But after a dare, one fifth former confessed to all of these 'sins' and was promptly ordered to dip his cock into cold water first thing in the morning and last thing at night!

So we knew what to expect when he cleared his throat and began droning on about the evils of 'the solitary vice'. 'Beware of this insidious disease which is the work of the devil,' he trumpeted. 'It cheats semen getting its full chance of making up the strong, manly chap you would otherwise be. Do not be tempted to throw away the seed that has been handed down to you as a sacred trust instead of keeping it and ripening it for bringing a son to you when you are fully matured.

'My advice to you all is this. Whenever you feel the impure urge coming on, say a prayer such as "Oh God, give me strength to resist the evil afflicting my body." I also recommend cold baths and long walks to help save yourself from this terrible scourge.'

'A final warning to you all – many of our finest doctors have written that, as surely as night follows day, self-abuse will lead to weak eye-sight, poor hearing and even insanity in later life. [*Unbelievable as this sounds to modern readers, Reverend Clarke was hardly exaggerating. It was only until after the Great War that medical opinion stopped preaching that masturbation was immoral because it wasted valuable sperm needed to make healthy babies! – Editor.*] So take heed and make a promise to yourselves that you will resist the forces of darkness.'

He burbled on for a few more minutes and Harry Price-Bailey, an athletic fellow and a good friend of both Frank and myself, grunted: 'I suppose that will keep us from pulling our puds for at least five minutes!'

For several years after I left St Lionel's I was especially cross with Dr Keeleigh for letting this clerical lunatic fill the minds of ignorant boys with such nonsense – and I don't care who says anything to the contrary, I'm damned sure that a five-knuckle shuffle never harmed anyone. I rest my case on no other grounds that if Reverend Clarke's view was correct, there'd be a bloody big demand for glasses and hearing-trumpets, that's for sure!

Any notice that might have been taken of the chaplain's words had gone by the evening, for that night, after lights out in the dormitory, Frank and I told our form-mates all about the excitements of our holiday. As we expounded in graphic detail about the several ways we had fucked Diana, Cecily, Sally and Polly, the lot of us soon sported gigantic hard-ons including Frank and myself! Within a minute, all the boys brought out their pricks and tossed themselves off, Frank and myself included. The experience was hardly unpleasant but since I had tasted the joys of a genuine fuck, I found that taking oneself in hand is fine as far as it goes but is only the first step on the road to sexual fulfilment.

I woke with the dawn the next morning and decided to go for an early morning run round Blodgett's Field, where football and cricket fixtures were played against other schools. Running before breakfast was a practice encouraged by Dr

Keeleigh but not to excess for it was banned during the winter months. I rummaged through my locker and put on my athletic vest and shorts and went down the stairs as quietly as possible as I did not wish to wake up others who were still asleep. As I made my way out towards the front door I heard two of the servant girls who came in daily from the nearby village talking. I recognised the dulcet tones of Melanie, perhaps the prettiest and certainly the girl who was most often drooled over by the older boys. It was rumoured that she had gone for a walk with Claridge of the Modern Sixth Senior who had boasted that she had let him slide his hand inside her blouse. But most of us, perhaps from envy, did not believe him!

I strained my ears and heard Melanie say: 'Yes, Dolly, so there we were, just the two of us in the changing room. Well, I didn't know at first that Geoffrey had gone in to take a shower, I thought the place was empty.'

'My, my, so it's Geoffrey now, is it,' said Dolly, her companion, with a laugh. 'It's plain Mister Ormondroyd to the likes of me and the rest of the girls!' My heart missed a beat – they were talking about my history master, a young man who had recently joined the school after leaving University. He had obtained his post at St Lionel's because Dr Keeleigh was always keen to keep a balance in the staff between youth and experience.

'Oh, go on with you,' said Melanie. 'Do you want to hear what happened or not? Yes? Well, I went in and heard Geoffrey singing in the shower I decided to stay around, especially when I saw his clothes lying in a heap on the floor. I peeped into the shower room and I saw him standing with his back to me under the shower, turning himself slowly round under the water jets, massaging the soap into his muscular body. What a fine figure of a man he is, Dolly, such a broad chest and such pinchable firm bum cheeks! When he turned round to the front I could take a long hard look at his big cock and it was so exciting when he soaped his shaft and it bounced up in his hand into the stiffest white truncheon you could ever wish to see! I don't mind telling you that my pussey started to dampen and I put down my mop and slipped my hand inside my blouse to rub my titties, which were already tingling unbearably as Geoffrey played with his prick, not knowing that an eager pair of eyes was watching his every move!

'So what did you do about it?' prompted Dolly, laughing lewdly as she sat down on the stairs to hear the end of the anecdote.

'What do you think!' retorted Melanie, sitting down beside her. 'I went back to the changing room and bolted the door. Then I took off my blouse and skirt and stood there with just my knickers on waiting for Geoffrey to come out. I didn't have to wait long and he was even more ready for action than I was, being stark naked except for a towel with which he was wiping his face. His cock looked heavy and juicy, swinging between his thighs so he couldn't have brought himself off in the shower, I thought to myself, which would help things along.

' "My God, Melanie, how did you get in here?" he gasped, hastily draping the towel round his waist.

"I wondered if I might have some private instruction in indoor games." I said boldly, stepping towards him and pushing my body up against his. I could feel his prick rising as I reached down and pulled down the towel, letting his swollen tool jump up to stand high against his tummy. I put my hands on his shoulders and pushed them downwards. He made no resistance as we sank to the floor and I thrust my titties in his face. He sucked them up marvellously as I clasped his massive cock and began to wank him. He then worked his hands inside my knickers and rubbed my pussey with the flat of his hand before he pulled down my knickers. Then he did something that's never happened to me before ... he leaned down and pushed my knickers over my ankles and then screwed them up in his hand and began rubbing the bundle against my soaking pussey! He made a sheath for his finger with the wet knickers and frigged my cunney with it. He wiggled his finger to the hilt until my knicks were saturated with my love juice. Then he eased them off his finger and frigged me with his bare fingers.

'So I wriggled myself around to bring my face up to his throbbing prick. I popped my lips over the crown of his cock and curled my tongue around his helmet, licking away whilst I cupped his tight ballsack. But I wanted him to fuck me so I only tongued the tip of his knob before lying down on my back. "Push that big dick in my cunt," I said and he didn't need asking twice! He slipped that fat bulb in my cunney. I came straightaway and could feel the juice running out of me, clinging to my pussey hairs as his cock crashed through my love channel. He kept

194

ramming his well-greased tool until we were both screaming in delight until he filled me with his sticky spunk. We lay together and his shaft stayed hard inside me as I felt his sperm trickle out of my cunt and down over my thighs. I would have liked to have continued but it was neither the time nor the place. I had to finish my work and Geoffrey was the duty master at breakfast so we both went into the shower to refresh ourselves and got dressed again as quickly as we could.'

'Are you going to see Mr Ormondroyd, oh, sorry, I mean Geoffrey, again?'

'I should say so! We've arranged to meet in his study tomorrow night at ten o'clock, I can't wait, Dolly! It's been three months since I've had a good fuck!'

I waited for the two girls to walk away before continuing my descent. Melanie's story had given me a huge stiffstander but I took Reverend Clark's advice and went for a brisk early-morning job instead of finishing myself off with a five-knuckle shuffle. It wasn't the chaplain and his dire warnings of perdition that stopped me relieving my feelings in the time-honoured fashion, but rather a gut feeling that somehow, somewhere, I was going to be involved in fucking. Since I was a small boy, my father had always told me to trust my instincts. I did so now, despite the total lack of credible evidence that might point to such a happy state of affairs. As it happens, such trust was not to be misplaced – though I would never have guessed in a million years just how such serendipity between fantasy and reality would be achieved!

I did, however, have to wait until the next day

for my dream to be realised. It all started when, as he had promised, Dr Keeleigh called Frank and myself to his study just before luncheon to meet Prince Salman – or, as the headmaster added, Salman Prince as he would be known at St Lionel's.

I liked the look of Salman from the moment we met – he was a tall, powerfully built chap with a firm handshake. 'Good to meet you, Mountjoy, and you too Folkestone,' he called cheerily. 'I hope I won't be a burden and I'm really grateful if you'll show me the ropes.'

At this point there was a tap on the door and, of all people, Melanie came in. 'You wanted to see me, sir,' she said and Dr Keeleigh asked her to show Salman where the laundry was situated, to explain how the household facilities of the school were run, and to take him back to the Fourth Form Common Room afterwards.

After they left Dr Keeleigh sat down in his superb red leather chair (donated a few years back by the Old Lionelsians on his fiftieth birthday) and said: 'There is just one further matter about which I want to speak to you. There may be, amongst some of the more vulgar of your form-mates or indeed other boys, a feeling of prejudice against our Indian Prince on the grounds of the colour of his skin. Any such foolishness is abhorrent in my eyes and in fact amongst the very highest in the land. ''Mislike me not for my complexion'' says the Moor in *The Merchant Of Venice* and it is an unfortunate fact that there will be those who may wish to make sneering remarks about Prince behind his back. If this happens, I want you to remind the offender that no less a person than His Majesty The King himself on a visit to India twenty five years ago berated some officials of the East India Company who spoke disparagingly about the natives. He told them that because man has a dark skin there is no reason why he should be treated like a brute.'

'Very good sir, but suppose someone says something out of place directly to the Prince himself?' ventured Frank.

A rare twinkled appeared in Dr Keeleigh's eyes. 'Ah, I don't think that will happen more than once,' he chuckled. 'I don't intend to broadcast the fact that Salman has taken lessons in fisticuffs from Harry Willoughby, the professional middle-weight boxing champion. He showed himself to be a willing pupil! I would rather wish you boys kept this information to yourselves and let anyone who tries to rag our new friend about his colour to find out for himself!'

After the last lesson of the day we took Salman to the study which he would share with Frank and myself. Coincidentally, we needed a third chap as our former studymate Nick Clee had left St Lionel's at the end of the summer term to join his parents in East Africa. [*Rupert must surely be referring here to Major Colonel Sir Nicholas Clee VC, DSO, the High Commissioner of Kenya and Uganda from 1917 to 1929 – Editor*].

'I suppose this room must be a bit spartan after your father's palace,' said Frank as he busied himself with putting on the kettle for tea. 'And I bet you had something a darned sight tastier than bread and butter and a slice of cake for tea.'

'Yes, I was spoiled rotten,' agreed Salman. 'But

as it says in your Bible: "Better a dinner of herbs where love is, than a stalled ox and hatred therein." ' We looked at him in awe. 'Proverbs, Chapter 15, verse 17.' he added kindly.

'I thought you worshipped those funny statues with lots of arms and sacred cows and all that sort of thing.' I said.

'No, no, my dear Rupert, my family are Moslems and you are talking of Hinduism. I don't know too much about their religion except that the cow is regarded as a symbol of Mother Earth which is why the animal is sacred and many of my Hindu friends are vegetarians,' he explained. 'Our holy book is the Koran though we do accept much of Jewish and Christian teaching.'

'Yes, we studied Mohammed and his teachings last term. What I remember best is that men are allowed more than one wife, aren't they?' said Frank.

'If you're a glutton for punishment,' returned Salman with a smile. 'I think that like my father I shall settle for just one but keep a harem of concubines for pleasure.'

I licked my lips. 'When were you allowed to . . . um –'

'Have my first woman?' said Salman, finishing the question for me. 'I had my first when I was thirteen. But that was quite unofficial and my father would have been furious, especially as the girl concerned was one of his favourites.' He paused and then, with a furrowed brow, he added in his perfect though slightly sing-song accented English: 'But since we're talking about this important subject, let me tell you that whilst I've been in England I have suffered from a grevious shortage of available bed-worthy females.

'But Miss Melanie, now, the girl who showed me round the school facilities before lunch, I would very much enjoy fucking her. My worry is that this might be against the rules of the school.'

Frank laughed out loudly. 'I don't see why, no-one's ever said anything against it. I would have thought a bigger worry was to persuade Melanie to come across.'

'Oh, that's no problem,' he said confidently.

'How do you know?' I demanded.

'Well, I've already asked her and she's coming here at half past eight this evening so we'll have an hour to enjoy ourselves before we have to go to bed.'

We stared at him in goggle-eyed astonishment. 'You asked her, just like that, if she wanted to be fucked and she immediately made an arrangement to see you tonight? My God, you're a fast worker. Perhaps your being a high-born foreign prince impressed her?'

But Salman shook his head. 'No, I don't really think so. I believe it is far more likely that she was impressed by my giving her half of this little piece of paper,' he commented, rummaging in his wallet to being out a carefully cut portion of a fifty pound note!

'Phew, I'll wager that Melanie hasn't seen too many of these,' I whistled. 'No, and I wonder if she's seen many of these either,' said Frank, giving his prick a suggestive circular rub with the palm of his hand.

'You don't think she is a virgin?' asked Salman anxiously.

'No, absolutely not,' I assured him firmly. I suddenly remembered that Melanie might have made an appointment with Salman this evening but that she had also made an assignation with Mr Ormondroyd for ten o'clock. 'She's no virgin, Salman,' I repeated and I told the boys what I had overheard on the stairs early this morning.

'Good,' said Salman with relief. 'I don't want any indignant fathers round here demanding that I marry their daughters and all that sort of nonsense. I shall enjoy myself tonight.'

We looked jealously at him as Frank poured the tea. 'Dash it, there's something else I'd better tell you,' he said.

'You've brought a girl from your dad's harem as well,' I sighed.

'No, no, old chap, it's about Melanie. I suggested that she bring two friends along tonight.'

'You jammy bugger!' grunted Frank enviously. 'Are you going to have three girls tonight?'

'I hope so,' he replied cheerfully. 'But my dear chaps, the other two ladies are primarily for your enjoyment.'

'For us?' I exclaimed.

'Most certainly,' said Salman courteously. 'I do hope I haven't offended you but I thought we would have a little party to celebrate my arrival at St Lionel's and who better to ask than my two new friends. Of course, if you prefer not to indulge yourselves, do let me know.'

'Oh we wouldn't dream of letting you down, would we, Rupert?' said Frank. 'Salman, old boy, we'd love to take part – I can see that we three are going to get along very well indeed!'

It was difficult to keep our minds on our homework but we did our best until the dinner bell rang out. We bolted through our meal and were back in our study by eight o'clock. I must say that Salman was very cool about the whole affair, but Frank and I could hardly keep still as we were so excited at the thought of a big sex party. In the end Salman turned to us and said: 'I say, you fellows, why not sit down and relax. The girls won't be here for another half an hour. Use the time like me to relax your mind and body. You'll be in much better shape if you can try a spot of meditation.'

We followed his advice but in my mind's eyes I could picture Melanie's large white breasts with the pink rosebud titties and I let myself drool about how I would run my hands over those gorgeous globes and then let them rove across her belly to that curly growth of cunney hair which curled in rich, dark locks in a triangle between her legs, tapering to a tantalising thinness where her pouting pussey lips would be waiting for my sturdy shaft.

Naturally, these lewd thoughts made my prick swell up as I sat in my armchair so I propelled the chair round with my bottom so that it faced away from the others. My cock was now pushing up uncomfortably in my lap so I unbuttoned my trousers to accommodate my stiffstander which stood proudly to attention as I capped and uncapped the bulging red knob in my hand.

I was so engrossed in this reverie that I did not notice Salman standing by me. 'I don't think Melanie and her friends will be disappointed by that rampant weapon,' he said admiringly.

'You should see Frank's, it's massive compared to mine,' I warned him.

'Bigger than this?' he asked and he took out his bulging brown tool out of his trousers. There was something different about his prick which at first I could not make out. But then when he began pulling his hand up and down his throbbing shaft I realised what was so strange about it – there was no foreskin to pull back from his bare knob!

My curiosity must have showed on my face for Salman enquired: 'Is something wrong?'

'No, no, it's just that I have never seen a prick like yours before,' I said hastily.

Frank came across to look and Salman said, 'Oh yes, of course, neither of you can be circumcised. Did you not know that, like the Jews, followers of the Prophet have our foreskins removed when we are small?' [*Circumcision did not become fashionable in Britain until the 1930s when it was widely practiced amongst the upper classes. Since the 1960s it has lost much of its popularity in Europe although the operation is still very much favoured in America. It remains, of course, a fundamental observance even amongst secular Jews and Muslims – Editor.*]

Frank showed Salman his giant whopper and, to my chagrin, my old pal's penis again took the top honours! But then there was a knock on the door and we hastily crammed our pricks away. As it transpired, we need not have been too concerned for it was none other than Melanie, who had arrived a little early along with two girls who I had never seen before. They turned out to be friends of hers from Lord Nutley's big country house which was only a mile or so away. 'These are my friends Lucy and Tricia,' said Melanie brightly, pointing to two very attractive young girls of about eighteen. Lucy was a full-figured female whose pert, pretty face was encircled by a mob of blonde curls whilst Tricia was of a dark complexion, more slender of figure but with well proportioned breasts which thrust proudly against her tight-fitting blouse. We introduced ourselves and Salman asked: 'May I offer you ladies a drink?'

'Thank you, that would be very nice,' said Melanie and I watched in amazement as the hospitable Indian produced a bottle of brandy from his locker.

'I'm sorry there's no champagne,' he apologised, 'but we don't yet have an ice-box in our study. Rupert, remind me to ask Dr Keeleigh tomorrow if I can have one sent in.'

He poured generous measures for all of us though he abstained (his religion forbidding the consumption of alcohol). We polished off the bottle between us without his help! This loosened any inhibitions and we were soon paired off, each boy sitting in an armchair with a girl on his knee. Frank had made a beeline for Tricia from the very beginning of these proceedings and Melanie was cuddling up closely to Salman, which left me with my arms around Lucy, a fate I happily succumbed to as, though I would not have spurned any of these fine women, Lucy would have been my prick's first choice!

'This new electric light is much too bright,' complained Melanie with a pretended petulance. 'Who'll be a good boy and turn it off?' Frank nobly volunteered and I called out quietly:

'And while you're there, turn the key in the lock, old chap.'

There was still enough light coming in from the corridor for us to see what we were about – and as soon as Frank settled down in the armchair all three couples began to snog passionately. I was too busy engaging in a burning kiss with Lucy to see what the others were doing but I could see that Melanie was already half-naked, her discarded blouse by Salman's feet. When I removed Lucy's top I discovered to my delight that she was not wearing anything underneath it. So I cupped her lovely bare breasts in my hands as our tongues frantically searched each other's mouths until I thought my poor straining cock would burst! But then this delicious girl slipped from my arms and, standing in front of me, she kicked off her shoes and undid her skirt, letting it fall to the ground. She peeled off her brief white panties and in no time at all stood there fully nude, obviously enjoying to the full the way I was goggling at her beauty. She caressed her own heavy breasts with their dark raised nipples and stood directly in front of me so that her curly blonde bush was staring me full in the face. I kissed the snowy plain of her belly and then ran my lips lower, through the strands of her silky thatch. My hands circled round her glorious buttocks as I buried my head between her thighs and drew her against me. My tongue crept down her slit which was nice and moist. More by luck than judgement (for remember, dear reader, just how inexperienced I was at this age) I found her clitty almost at once and Lucy gasped as I found

204

her magic button and started to roll my tongue around the erectile piece of flesh.

'Aaaah, that's lovely, you've made me spend already,' she moaned quietly. 'But now let me see what you have between your legs to offer me, as you're much younger than my boyfriend.' She expertly unbuttoned my flies and my naked penis sprung out to pay its respects. She wanked my cock with an amused look on her face and her wet, pink tongue flicked out to lick her lips. 'You're better endowed than I expected,' she admitted as she rubbed her hands round my pulsating prick. Then she bent down on her knees and encircled the tip of my helmet with her lips which made me groan with delight.

'Be quiet, you two, we don't want to be disturbed by any visitors,' hissed Frank so I gritted my teeth and leaned back in my chair as Lucy started to suck my knob lustily, licking and lapping as her soft fingers tickled my balls. She moved her lips and tongue up and down, each time taking more of my tool into her throat. This excited my prick so much that all I could do was to hiss out the first words of warning as I shot my hot spunky jism into the back of her throat. I withdrew my still swollen cock from her mouth and she took hold of it in her hand again as she jumped onto my lap. We peered across in the dim light and I could see that Melanie and Salman had wasted no time – she had leaned over the arm of their chair and Salman was fucking her doggie-style, whipping his thick brown prick into the glistening moist crack of her cunt from behind and slapping her bum cheeks lightly with every thrust forwards as he jerked his hips to and fro.

'Oh, what joy! Oh, what bliss!' cried Salman as he happily pushed his prick in and out of Melanie's squelchy slit. He held her round the waist until he was completely embedded and then shifted his hand round to fondle her superbly uptilted breasts, rubbing the pink titties until they were as erect as his cock which was nestling in her juicy cunt. His entire body quivered as he withdrew almost fully before pushing home, sheathing his cock so fully at each stroke that his balls banged against her rounded little bum cheeks. Melanie turned her head and waggled her backside. 'Harder! Fuck me harder!' she whispered fiercely. 'I'm coming, oh, I'm coming, oh, oh, OH' and she let out a screech of ecstacy as she shuddered to her climax. As she spurted her love juices Salman sent spouts of spunk flooding into her cunney, while he gave her lovely bum cheeks a final smack. He stayed still, however, with his cock still enclosed in her sopping crack.

'My, your prick's still nice and stiff. Can you carry on?' said Melanie hopefully.

'Certainly I can,' said Salman and he began gently to pull his gleaming shaft out from between her bum cheeks. His cock was still rock hard and he started to fuck Melanie more slowly this time. As Lucy rubbed up my own stiff staff, we turned our attention to Frank and Tricia. They were kissing rapturously and Frank had taken off all of her clothes, giving us an excellent view of Tricia's exquisite young breasts which were lusciously rounded, as white as alabaster and capped with superbly fashioned hard tawny nipples which were surrounded by large circled aureoles. 'Kiss my titties, Frank, they adore being made love to,' panted the adorable girl and Frank wasted no further time. He licked and nipped those lovely rubbery raspberries, running his hands along her thighs. The trembling girl turned sideways so that Frank could insert his hands between her legs and explore her pussey, which was thatched with a delicate covering of jet black hair. She moved across and over him so that her pussey was above his face as she lowered her head to kiss his throbbing tool. Her soft hands caressed his heavy balls as with a sensual slowness she slicked her tongue up and down the length of his thick shaft, taking her time to reach the red mushroomed helmet which was twitching frantically as she finally coated it with the tip of her pink tongue. Then she suddenly engulfed his shining knob, sliding down his foreskin and gobbling greedily on her fleshy lollipop.

Frank's tongue was now pressed against her pussey and he licked at her dripping crack, moving around the outer lips and gently slipping his tongue inside the rolled lips until the juices flowed into his open mouth.

My own cock was now quivering with unrequited lust but (as she told me later) though she would have loved me to fuck her again, Lucy kindly decided to offer my tool to Tricia who loved threesomes but rarely had the opportunity to indulge herself.

Lucy murmured: 'Why don't you fuck Tricia's bottom, Rupert? I know she'd really enjoy that very much.' I hesitated for a moment but the sweet girl pulled me up by my cock and brought me round to the armchair where Tricia was sucking Frank's cock whilst he licked out her cunney. She had one leg over the chair and the other over Frank and the firm, curvaceous cheeks of her bum were spread out deliciously, giving me an excellent view of her wrinkled brown rear dimple. Lucy released my cock to bring forward the chair from my desk which I knelt upon to enable me to lean over Tricia and wedge my cock between her glorious buttocks. Then the thoughtful girl pulled me back and washed my knob with saliva before taking hold of my shaft and aiming my knob at Tricia's winking little rosette which beckoned me so alluringly. She eased my glowing crown between those gorgeous bottom cheeks which I fairly ached to split with my iron hard cock. Her work soon achieved the desired effect. My shaft enveloped itself beautifully between the rolling buttocks until it was fully ensconced in her warm, tight bum and I leaned over Tricia's gleaming body to play with her luscious breasts.

I worked in and out of her arse very slowly at first but then, as Tricia artfully waggled her bottom provocatively, at a faster pace, pushing my entire body backwards and forwards, making Tricia's divinely proportioned bum cheeks slap loudly against my belly. I screwed up my eyes in sheer bliss but opened them again with a gasp as I felt Lucy's hands pressing against my thighs. The lewd sight of Tricia's cunney and bottom being pleasured at the same time had fired Lucy so intensely that she now knelt behind me and thrust her head between my legs. She took my ballsack into her mouth, moving her head in time with my thrusts.

Salman and Melanie now joined us and I turned round to see the young prince position himself on his back so that his head was directly underneath Lucy's cunt. She raised herself to accommodate him and then with a squeal of joy lowered her enticing golden cunney onto his lips and he noisily nuzzled into her golden honeypot, flicking his tongue into the soft folds of her juicy pussey. Melanie was now down on her knees beside them and straddling his body, holding open her pink cunney lips as she sat firmly upon his stiff penis, sitting with her luscious buttocks towards him while she rode up and down his delighted pole. Salman grasped her bottom cheeks with both hands and squeezed them rhythmically as she pushed up and down, contracting her powerful pussey muscles with every downwards movement, to their joint delight. At the same time she reached between his legs and took his balls in her hand and began to jiggle them, scraping the hairy sack with the fingernails until Salman was crooning with delight.

This was my first multiple fuck and I must confess that it was most stimulating to see all those fine cocks and cunnies in action. All three of us boys came closely together, Frank jetting his spunk into Tricia's mouth whilst I spurted my sperm into her bottom and Salman sent up a stream of jism into Melanie's cunt. The girls, too, all achieved copious climaxes, especially Lucy whose love juices poured into Salman's mouth as he swallowed her tangy spendings.

There was just time for one more fucking chain.

This time Melanie sucked me off whilst Frank fucked her as he lapped at Lucy's titties whilst Salman was diddling her pussey at the same time as he plunged his prick into Tricia's sopping cunt, with Tricia completing the circle by finger-fucking Melanie's bum. We would have liked to have changed positions for yet a further joust but it was approaching the time when Melanie had arranged to meet Mr Ormondroyd. So Salman passed the second half of the fifty pound note to Melanie with our grateful thanks as the girls began to dress.

'Thank you very much,' panted Melanie as she buttoned up her skirt, 'we must do this again next week. And this time, you don't have to bring your wallet. It's been a pleasure to fuck with such vigorous young gentlemen, hasn't it, girls?'

'I should say so,' echoed Tricia. 'It would be grand to spend the night together, wouldn't it?' Lucy agreed and said she was free any night next week and that we could use her cousin Amanda's house as her parents would be away. 'You'll have to find another boy for her, of course, but I'm sure that can be easily arranged.'

'No problems there,' said Frank cheerily and we kissed the girls good-night. We were in the dormitory spot on time at ten o'clock but perhaps I was over-fatigued by all the fucking for I simply could not get to sleep. So I quietly got out of bed and slipped on my dressing gown to fetch a book from our study. Like many other boys, I also had a torch which I used to read in the dark.

I kept the study in darkness as I searched the bookshelves for it was strictly against the rules to leave the dormitory after lights out. I found the book I was looking for, a ripping adventure story by Tom Shackleton, my favourite author, when I was startled by the opening of the door. I spun round with a gasp to see the figure of Melanie framed in the door.

'Gosh, you gave me a fright!' I said. She apologised and explained that she was missing a earring and hoped that one of us might have discovered it on the floor. 'I'm afraid not,' I said quietly. 'I wouldn't mind helping you to look for it now but I'm not supposed to be here so I can't put on the light.'

'Never mind, it wasn't a very expensive one and perhaps you'll find it in the morning. But what are you doing here anyway?'

I explained how I could not sleep and Melanie said: 'Well, Mr Ormondroyd won't be coming round looking for you, that's for sure. I've left him fast asleep in his bed!'

'Is he good between the sheets?' I asked.

'Oh yes, I've no complaints but don't worry, you silly boy, I was more than satisfied with the way that you and your friends performed – especially the lad with that monster cock, what's his name, Frank Folkestone! Still, Geoffrey – that's Mr Ormondroyd – knows how to use his tackle. We wasted no time and as soon as I got to his room I sat on the bed, fondling his stiff cock through his trousers which he unbuttoned for me to let his tadger shoot out like a coil. He sat down beside me and worked his hand down to my muff which was already damp with all the spendings from you. He moved his fingers between the edges of my crack as we kissed and I wrapped my legs around his hand as I lowered my head to suck his cock.

' "Let's continue this in bed,' he said and so we undressed and snuggled up together. As we embraced I felt his hard tool press against my tummy and then he rolled me over on to my back and pressed his helmet through my pussey lips. I was really enjoying myself as with a deep groan he thrust his strong shaft straight in and his balls slapped against my bum. I lifted my bottom up to get as much of him inside me as possible. I wrapped my legs round his back and clawed his shoulders with my fingernails as he started to pump his rod in and out of my squishy pussey. It took only a few strokes before I was twisting away like crazy. His cock seemed to swell inside my cunney and I spent first, soaking his shaft with my juices. Then I felt his whole frame shiver and he flooded my cunt with a spurt of hot spunk so huge that I could imagine it splashing against the rear walls of my love box. There was so much jism that my thighs were lathered as he pulled out his cock and rubbed it in my sticky cunney hair.

'He rolled off me, heaving and panting with exhaustion and said: "What a succulent little cunney you have there, Melanie. It sucked in my cock so sweetly that I'm spoiled now for any other." '

'You should think yourself honoured! He never compliments anyone in class, and I don't think he has much of a sense of humour,' I said with a gloomy laugh.

'Oh I don't know about that,' said Melanie, who somehow now found herself in my arms in one of the armchairs we had used for our escapade earlier in the evening. 'I said to him that

I had to really stretch my legs to accommodate thick pricks like his and do you know what he said? "Don't complain, Melanie – have you heard the rhyme about the girl who was worried about that? No? Well it goes like this:

There was a young lady from Harrow,
Who complained that her crack was too narrow,
For times without number,
She'd use a cucumber,
But could never accomplish a marrow."

'And it was just after he'd finished reciting this poem when something quite extraordinary happened ...'

[TO BE CONTINUED]

EROTIC CLASSICS FROM
CARROLL & GRAF

☐ Anonymous/AUTOBIOGRAPHY OF A FLEA $3.95
☐ Anonymous/CAPTURED $4.50
☐ Anonymous/CONFESSIONS OF AN ENGLISH MAID $4.50
☐ Anonymous/THE CONSUMMATE EVELINE $4.95
☐ Anonymous/THE EDUCATION OF A MAIDEN $4.50
☐ Anonymous/THE EROTIC READER $4.50
☐ Anonymous/THE EROTIC READER II $3.95
☐ Anonymous/THE EROTIC READER III $4.50
☐ Anonymous/THE EROTIC READER IV $4.95
☐ Anonymous/THE EROTIC READER V $4.95
☐ Anonymous/FALLEN WOMAN $4.50
☐ John Cleland/FANNY HILL $4.95
☐ Anonymous/FANNY HILL'S DAUGHTER $3.95
☐ Anonymous/FORBIDDEN PLEASURES $4.95
☐ Anonymous/HAREM NIGHTS $4.95
☐ Anonymous/INDISCREET MEMOIRS $4.50
☐ Anonymous/A LADY OF QUALITY $3.95
☐ Anonymous/LAY OF THE LAND $4.50
☐ Anonymous/LEDA IN BLACK ON WHITE $4.95
☐ Anonymous/MAID AND MISTRESS $4.50
☐ Anonymous/THE MERRY MENAGE $4.50
☐ Anonymous/SATANIC VENUS $4.50
☐ Anonymous/SWEET CONFESSIONS $4.50
☐ Anonymous/TROPIC OF LUST $4.50
☐ Anonymous/VENUS IN INDIA $3.95
☐ Anonymous/WHITE THIGHS $4.50

Available from fine bookstores everywhere or use this coupon for ordering.

THE FEMININE TOUCH
FROM CARROLL & GRAF